Mea

Book 8

The Sleepover

Katrina Kahler and Charlotte Birch

Table of Contents

Chapter One - Too Perfect

As Sydney's house came into view, Remmy and Sandy both gaped through the car window.

Remmy had thought that their home was big (especially in comparison to her house back in Sweet Lips) but Sydney's was at least double its size. It had more windows than she could possibly count and there was an elaborate pebbled driveway that was lined with circular pink rose bushes.

'Well, isn't this just lovely.' Janice turned around and looked at the girls. 'You must both be very excited?'

'Personally, I think it's a bit too showy,' Sandy huffed. 'And what's with all of the roses?'

'I think that the rose bushes are very beautiful, I bet they smell divine.'

'Whatever!' Sandy slumped down into her seat.

'It is a bit OTT,' Marcus commented.

'Nonsense, it's lovely. Sydney's father must have a very well-paid job.'

'Or he has rich parents,' Marcus said under his breath.

'What was that?' Janice looked at him.

'Nothing darling.' He gave her a forced smile.

Remmy clamped her mouth shut to try and stop herself from laughing. She couldn't deny that Sydney's house was impressive but her favorite place to live would always be their home back in Sweet Lips. She believed that it wasn't the size of a house that was important but the memories that were created within it.

They drove up to the front of the house and parked up behind Bridget's mom's dented Ford Fiesta. They all stepped out of the vehicles and Remmy and Janice both stared up at the enormous house.

'Hi, guys!' Bridget waved as she skipped her way over to them.

'Hi, Bridge!' Remmy beamed at her.

'Hello, Bridget.' Janice smiled at her. 'Hi June, isn't it a lovely day?' She walked over to Bridget's mom, who was still standing by her car.

Rachel's dad parked up behind Marcus's car and Rachel and Susie jumped out of it and excitedly rushed over to Sandy.

'Wow, I didn't realize that she was so super rich,' Rachel commented.

'It's amazing.' Susie craned her neck back so that she could peer higher.

'It's not that big,' Sandy muttered, as she folded her arms.

The extra-large, oak front door opened and Sydney and her parents walked out and greeted them.

'Hello everyone, it's so good to see you all,' Sydney's mom swished her long hair behind her back. 'I'm Catherine and this is my husband, Martin,' she gestured to the smartly dressed man who stood a step behind her.

'Hi.' He lifted up his hand in greeting.

'The word is hello, you know how I feel about abbreviated words,' she hissed at him. 'It's so lovely to have you all here. Sydney's been so excited, it's all she has talked about for the past week, isn't it Sydney?'

'Yeah.' Sydney looked at the floor.

'Yes.' Catherine glared at her.

'You really do have a lovely home,' Janice replied.

'It's not quite as lavish as our penthouse in New York was but I suppose it will do for now.'

'So, Martin, do you work locally?' Marcus asked.

Martin was about to reply but Catherine rudely stepped in front of him.

'Come in girls.' She gestured them forward.

All of the kids exchanged excited looks (including Sandy who couldn't hide the fact that she was actually really impressed by Sydney's house) before they waved goodbye to the adults and then stepped into the house.

'So, we'll pick them up at half-past ten tomorrow morning?' Bridget's mom asked.

'Yes, doll.' Catherine swished her hair. 'I can assure you all that your kids are in safe hands.'

The parents said their goodbyes and then they left the mansion. All of the girls stepped into the foyer and looked around open-mouthed. There was a marble floor, a glass spiral staircase with a bronze banister and there was a massive chandelier hanging from the ceiling.

'I hope that doesn't fall down.' Bridget pointed up to it as she whispered to Remmy.

Remmy gave a nervous giggle. She'd never seen a chandelier before, nor had she ever seen a house with such a massive foyer. It may have been beautifully decorated but it didn't feel homely. She looked down at her sweaty sneakers and hoped that Sydney and her mom didn't notice them.

'Sydney, you should go and show your friends where they're sleeping tonight and let them put down their bags. Then it'll be time for dinner.'

'Okay, Mom.' Sydney forced a smile. 'Follow me, you're going to love my room.'

Remmy hugged her bag as she followed Sydney up the spiral staircase.

'Your house is the biggest I've ever been in,' Bridget said, sounding awestruck.

'Yeah, it's huge,' Rach said.

'I suppose so. I mean, I know it is far bigger than all of your houses,' she smirked.

'How many bedrooms do you have?' Sandy asked.

'There are six and they all have ensuite bathrooms, of

course.'

'Sharing a bathroom is the worst. I have to wait for ages in the morning,' Bridget commented.

'Luckily, I don't have that problem.' Sydney stuck her nose ever so slightly into the air.

'Well, apart from at camp,' Bridget chuckled.

They followed Sydney along the wide, gold-leafed wallpapered corridor. Various pictures decorated the walls, including one of Catherine posing on the beach in shades and a big floppy hat. Remmy noticed that there weren't any pictures of Sydney or her dad on display and she thought that this was odd. Sydney came to a stop in front of a door near the end of the corridor.

'So, this is my bedroom.' She pushed open the door and stepped into the room.

The other girls followed her inside and all of them looked around awestruck. Her room was at least three times the size of any of theirs, there was a four-poster-bed with soft pink netting around it and in the far corner of the room, there was an oak dressing table that was covered in makeup. On the floor were five mattresses, all of them made up with crisp white sheets and fluffy cream blankets.

'Whoa,' Sandy said, as she rushed over to look at Sydney's makeup collection.

'Be careful with those, they're all very expensive,' Sydney said to her.

'So, what do you think?' Sydney asked as she smirked at Bridget and Remmy.

'It's amazing and I love the color scheme.' Bridget peered

around at the pastel pink and white room.

'I think I'm going to have it changed soon, I'm getting kinda bored with these colors.'

Rach and Susie had joined Sandy over by the makeup table. They were all inspecting the eyeshadows and sniffing the variety of flavored lip balms.

Remmy and Bridget sat down on mattresses next to each other. 'Syd's house is so cool,' Bridget said.

'I don't know if I like it...it doesn't feel very homely. It's lacking warmth or something,' Remmy remarked quietly.

'Right,' Bridget snorted. 'Anyways, I wonder what we're having for dinner? I hope it's a pizza.'

'I don't think it'll be pizza,' Remmy chuckled.

'It won't be.' Sydney appeared next to them. 'My mom would NEVER eat pizza.'

'Like never?' Bridget asked.

'Yeah, never. She's very health conscious.'

'She does look amazing. She's like a film star,' Bridget said.

'I guess.' Sydney shrugged. 'Anyway, dinner should be ready now.'

She strode over to the other girls and snatched her cherry-red lip gloss off Rach.

'That's expensive.' She glared at Rach before applying the lip-gloss to her lips and then puckered them. 'Let's downstairs for dinner, my parents don't like to be kept waiting.'

Sandy exchanged looks with the rest of the vampires before they followed Sydney out of her massive bedroom. On their way to the dining room, Sydney pointed at different rooms and told them what was in there...a theatre room, a gym, and a sauna room. She told them that she'd give the full tour after dinner. Bridget still had an awestruck look on her face. Every time Sydney pointed out a new room, Bridget excitedly clapped her hands together as she looked at Remmy.

Remmy forced a smile back, as she didn't want to burst her best friend's bubble. Even though she couldn't deny that Sydney's home was beautiful, she still felt that it was lacking something.

They walked into the dining room and all the visiting girls gasped. The room was large enough to fit a long, expensive looking table in it. The table was covered with a beautiful white tablecloth and highly polished gold cutlery. Sydney's parents were already sitting down, with her mom sitting at the head of the table.

Catherine smiled at them. 'Come in girls and take a seat.'

They all hurried to take a seat. It reminded Remmy of the dining rooms they had in Disney films. Nothing about it seemed real.

'This is amazing,' Bridget whispered to her.

Remmy gave a nod of her head. She'd lost count of how many times she'd heard Bridget use the word 'amazing' since they'd arrived here. She peered up at the other end of the table, it seemed so far away...as if it could have been in a separate room altogether. She imagined what it would be like if Sydney's family were the only ones sitting there. Would the parents still sit at either end of the table and Sydney somewhere in between? There's no way they could talk about their day unless they yelled.

'Girls, are you having a good time?' Catherine asked.

'Yes, thank you. Your house really is beautiful,' Rach said.

'Yes, it's amazing,' Bridget commented.

Remmy looked down at the table...smiling to herself.

'Good,' Catherine said with a pleased expression.

She looked behind her and clicked her fingers. A short, middle-aged woman, with her dark hair tied into a neat bun, hurried into the room. She was wearing a black dress with a crisp white apron tied around her waist. She was pushing a silver trolley full of delicate looking food. Just before she reached the table, she tripped on the leg of Remmy's chair and the food on the tray jolted forward.

'Maria, stop being so clumsy!' Catherine glared at her.

'Sorry Miss.' Maria blushed as she lifted a plate off the trolley and carefully placed it down in front of Catherine.

'I'm sorry, that was my fault,' Remmy apologised, looking embarrassed.

Catherine looked at Remmy and raised her perfectly shaped eyebrows. Eventually, she spoke, 'Don't be silly, you are a guest, Maria should know better.'

The maid lowered her eyes. She hurried back-and-forth from the trolley as she served the others and then she pushed the empty trolley out of the room. The girls looked down at their food. The large white plate had a few spears of asparagus tied together with parma ham and it was resting on a bed of leaves.

'What is this?' Bridget whispered to Remmy.

10

Remmy shook her head, she'd never eaten anything like this before. She looked over at Sydney and noticed that she'd cut off a tiny piece of asparagus before she put it into her mouth. She did the same, and as she chewed on the food she realized that it tasted good. She quickly ate the rest of it and then eagerly waited for the next course. The maid brought out a fish soup next and Remmy tried her best to eat it without spilling any of it onto the immaculately white linen tablecloth.

Martin dripped some of the soup onto his white shirt and Catherine immediately glared at him. He quickly dabbed at it with his napkin but she continued to look at him and then gave a slight shake of her head.

'So, girls, what activities do you have planned for tonight?' Her eyes were fixed on Sandy.

'Ahhh, I don't know,' Sandy blushed. 'I'd love to see more of your house, it's really beautiful.'

'Sydney, why haven't you given your friends a tour yet?' her mother frowned at her.

'I was going to, Mom.'

'Yes, well you should have done it already,' her mother snapped and then delicately brought a half-full spoon of soup to her mouth.

Bridget was trying her best not to slurp on the soup when her hand flinched and a big blob of cream-colored liquid landed on the tablecloth. She gave Remmy a horrified look and willed back tears. Catherine hadn't noticed yet, so Remmy quickly grabbed Bridget's bowl and moved it forward so that it covered the stain.

'Thank you,' Bridget mouthed to her and Remmy smiled

back.

The next course was grilled chicken with herb covered new potatoes and baby carrots. The maid didn't say anything when she moved Bridget's bowl and saw the stain, in fact, she positioned the plate of food down on the table so that it was covering it. There was an awkward silence as they all ate; the only sounds were the scraping of cutlery and chewing.

Remmy found herself trying to cut up her food and chew more quietly. Back in Sweets Lips when she'd stayed over at her friend's house they'd had hotdogs and she hadn't worried when she spilled ketchup on her arm. Back there, the atmosphere had been relaxed but here it was far more formal and terribly uncomfortable. She longed to be able to stick her grilled chicken in the middle of a bun and cover it in ketchup then eat it with her hands.

'That was delicious as always,' Catherine said to Maria as she cleared away her plate. 'Please give my compliments to Gus.'

Maria gave a nod of her head. 'I will pass on your compliment, Miss.'

'Would any of your girls like dessert?'

'Yes please,' Sydney said.

Catherine frowned at her. 'Are you sure? I think your waistline could do with a little break. We don't want you to get fat again...do we Sydney?'

'No.' She blushed, as she shook her head. 'I'm going to the bathroom." She pushed back her chair and hurried out of the room.

'So, would any of you like dessert?' Catherine smiled at

them.

The girls all exchanged looks with each other. They were all desperate to have dessert but after the way Catherine had spoken to Sydney, none of them wanted to ask for it.

'No one?' Catherine asked.

'No, thank you, I'm full,' Sandy said.

'It was delicious,' Susie remarked.

'Yes, amazing,' Bridget smiled.

'It was lovely. Please, can I be excused, I need to visit the bathroom?' Remmy asked awkwardly.

'Of course.'

Remmy pushed back her chair as quietly as she could and left the room. She stood in the corridor and looked around her. She didn't know where any of the bathrooms were but she thought she remembered the way back to Sydney's bedroom, so she decided to go there. She grabbed onto the bronze banister as she walked up the spiral staircase. Every picture that hung from the wall was perfectly straight, the walls didn't have any marks on them and she hadn't spotted one bit of dust or dirt. There weren't any faults to Sydney's home; not one. It was more like a show home than a place that was actually lived in.

She reached Sydney's bedroom and hurried across it and opened the bathroom door. Sydney was crouched over the toilet coughing. She looked up and spotted Remmy. Her eyes widened with shock and she quickly wiped her mouth with the back of her hand then stood up.

'W-what are you doing here?' Sydney glared at her.

'I'm sorry, I didn't know where any of the other bathrooms were. Are you okay? Are you sick? Do you need me to get your mom?'

'NO!' she shouted. 'No, you can't tell my mom.' She lowered her tone.

'Okay.'

'I mean it, Remmy, you can't tell anyone.'

'But if you're sick, I'm sure they'll understand.'

Sydney walked over to her, grabbed both of her arms and looked at her. 'Please Remmy, you can never tell anyone. I mean it! If you do...you'll destroy me.'

'I won't.'

'Do you promise?'

'Yeah, I promise.'

'Good, it can be our little secret.' Sydney forced a smile as she let go of Remmy's arms.

Remmy forced one back. She didn't understand what was going on. Why would Sydney care if people knew that she was ill? If Remmy felt sick she would have told her mom, so why was it such a big secret with Sydney? Still, it was obviously a big deal to her so she decided to keep her word and not say anything about it to anyone.

She left the room and sat down on her mattress, not knowing if she should go back downstairs again or stay where she was. Sydney washed her face and then joined Remmy in the bedroom.

'I'm so glad that you could all make it and that you all got to see my house.' She smiled at Remmy.

Sydney was acting like nothing had happened; like she hadn't been sick...so Remmy decided to go along with it. She didn't want to upset her host, not when she'd been kind enough to invite them all to sleep over.

'Thanks for inviting me, you'll have to stay at our place sometime,' Remmy said.

'That'd be great.' Sydney forced a smile.

The other girls returned to the bedroom in a whirlwind of excitement and immediately began to take over the bedroom. Sandy and the vampires went back over to the makeup table whilst Bridget examined the bookshelf that had some books, a few stuffed toys and a couple of china dolls on it. Remmy took her phone out of her bag and scrolled through FB on it. The room suddenly fell silent. Remmy looked up and saw that Catherine had just entered the room.

'Hi, girls,' Catherine placed her hand on her hip as she smiled at them. 'I'm here to collect your phones. I think it's important that you have a social-media-free night. Trust me, girls, you'll thank me for it.' She winked at them.

'But, what if someone tries to reach me?' Sandy sounded horrified.

'Then they'll just have to wait until tomorrow, won't they?' Catherine smirked.

'I suppose so.' Sandy sighed as she pulled her phone out of her pocket and reluctantly handed it over to Catherine.

Rach, Susie, and Sydney all handed their phones over. Remmy turned hers off before she held it out to Catherine. She didn't see why they couldn't have just turned their phones off, without having to hand them over. She didn't mention this though, as she didn't want to appear rude. Bridget quickly typed out a message to her mom...

> Everything's great. I'm going to bed early x.

'Your phone, too,' Catherine hoovered over her.

Bridget sighed as she held out her phone.

'Great, now I'll leave you girls to it.' She shimmied her way over to the door. 'Don't worry, I'll give them back to you in the morning. I'm sure you'll all survive until then.' She sniggered to herself as she walked out of the room.

'I'm sorry about that.' Sydney gave them an apologetic look. 'I know it totally sucks not having our phones.'

'It's okay.' Bridget gave her a slight smile.

'Great.' Remmy smiled back as she sat down on the floor in front of them. 'So, how much fun was camp?'

'It was fun, apart from the permanent marker above my lip. It took days for it to come off completely. My brother thought it was hilarious but I wasn't laughing.' Bridget remarked.

'I wonder who did it?' Remmy gave Sydney a suspicious look.

Sandy smirked.

'No idea, but when we find out who it was...we'll get them back.'

Yeah,' Remmy muttered. 'I loved camp. I really miss the activities and the hotdogs.'

'Yeah, the food was great.' Bridget licked her lips. 'The disco was fantastic too.'

'Yeah, everyone loves a disco,' Sandy said, as she led the vampires over to them.

'Yeah, I miss everything about camp,' Rach said.

'Me too,' Susie added.

Sydney smiled. 'Camp was great but my house is so much better.'

'Yeah, it is pretty impressive. Can we have that tour now?' Sandy asked.

'Soon. How about a game first?'

'What kind of game?' Sandy gave Sydney a skeptical look.

'How about truth or dare?' Sydney suggested.

'Okay, I'm asking first though,' Sandy smirked. 'Remmy, have you ever kissed Charlie?'

'You don't have to answer it,' Sydney piped in. 'You can pick dare if you'd prefer.'

'No, it's okay, I'll answer it.' Remmy blushed. 'He's only kissed me on the cheek.'

Sandy grinned and the vampires giggled. Remmy looked down at her feet, she'd never played this game before and she wasn't sure that she liked it very much.

'Charlie clearly adores Remmy, he just doesn't want to rush things,' Bridget said.

Sydney smiled. 'I think it's cute that he wants to be with you.'

'Thanks,' Remmy muttered. 'So, whose turn is next?'

'Mine.' Rach gave a sly smile. 'So, Bridget, do you have a crush on Colin?'

Bridget's face turned redder than her hair. She definitely didn't want to have to answer that question in front of the vampires.

'I pick dare.'

'Okay then,' Rach smirked. 'Sydney, can I use your laptop?'

'I guess so.' Sydney shrugged. She walked over to her desk, picked up her hot pink covered laptop and held it out to Rach.

'Be careful with it, it's almost brand new,' she said with a superior sounding voice.

'I will be.' Rach took it from her. 'Bridget, I dare you to log into your FB account and to send a message to Colin saying *hi*.'

'W-what?' Bridget stared at her open-mouthed.

'What's the big deal, you're friends, right?' Sandy smirked.

'Yeah, but I haven't messaged him on FB before.' Bridget was now the color of a beetroot.

'Are you going to chicken out?' Rach stared at her.

'No, of course not.' Bridget took the laptop from her. 'I'm doing it.'

She logged into her FB account and typed out the message *hi* to Colin. She floated her finger over the send button before eventually jabbing it.

Sydney glared at her. 'Be careful, that's a top of the range laptop.'

'Sorry.' Bridget blushed as she looked down at the message box.

What if he didn't reply? What if he made fun of her for sending it? Worse still, what if he thought that she was weird for sending it and never spoke to her again?

The laptop dinged and a message popped up. Everyone peered over Bridget's shoulders in an attempt to read it but she lowered the laptop lid far enough so the others couldn't see the screen.

> Hi Bridget! Wow, I can't believe that you're talking to me.

'What did lover boy say?' Sandy giggled.

'Did he turn you down?' Rach laughed.

'Embarrassing!' Susie grinned.

'He replied!' Bridget smiled.

'I would like my laptop back this year preferably, and for us to get on with the game.' Sydney folded her arms.

Feeling even more flustered, Bridget quickly typed out a smiley face and sent it to Colin before she logged out of her FB account and passed the laptop back to Sydney.

'My turn.' Sydney gave a sly smile as her eyes fixed on Sandy. 'Sandy, would you like Charlie to be your boyfriend?'

Sandy looked almost as horrified as Remmy had done. There was an awkward silence as Sandy deliberated on what to do.

'Dare,' she muttered.

'Okay then. I dare you to sneak into the kitchen and bring back something from the fridge.'

'I don't even know where the kitchen is. Besides, won't your chef be in there?'

'It's the room next to the dining room and no, Gus would have gone home by now. Look, if you're too afraid then you can always answer my question.'

'I'm not afraid. I'll do it.' Sandy jumped up to her feet. 'I'll be back soon,' she strode over to the door and tiptoed into the corridor.

Sydney grinned. 'This is going to be hilarious.'

'Why?' Remmy asked.

'Wait and see.'

The girls chatted to themselves as they waited for Sandy to return. Bridget found herself wondering what food Sandy would sneak out and she secretly hoped that it would be chocolate. A loud beeping sound echoed through the entire house and all the girls gave each other puzzled looks before they got up and followed Sydney over to the door. Lights throughout the house had turned on and a frantic Sandy was running up the stairs. She puffed her way into Sydney's room and closed the door behind her.

'What happened?' Rach asked.

'Yeah, what's going on?' Susie said.

'I could ask her the same question!' Sandy frowned at Sydney.

'No snacking, Sydney, you know the rules!' Catherine shouted from the corridor.

All of the girls looked at Sydney for answers.

She smirked. 'Okay, so there may be an alarm on the fridge.'

'What! Who has an alarm on their fridge?' Rach looked shocked.

'My mom's a massive control freak, she even controls the fridge and when it can be accessed.' Sydney dabbed at a tear in the corner of her eye. 'When I was younger I was quite overweight and mom hated that. She wants everyone and everything around her to be perfect and I wasn't, so she put me on a strict diet. She's terrified that I'll become fat again and embarrass her.'

'That's awful,' Bridget commented.

'Yeah, how can your mom be so cruel?' Rach asked, which caused Sandy to elbow her in the arm. 'Ouch!' She rubbed it.

'It's okay, I'm used to it,' Sydney sighed. 'Mom controls everything and everyone in this house. My father stopped thinking for himself many years ago.'

Sandy and the vampires raised their eyebrows. For once they were speechless. Remmy touched Sydney's shoulder and gave her a smile. Bridget tried to look sympathetic but she couldn't stop thinking about how awful it would be to have a controlling mom who put an alarm on the fridge. Remmy now understood why Sydney acted the way that she did. Her home life was controlled down to the smallest detail and she didn't have any power. So at school, she wanted to be an alpha girl and have things her own way. Maybe Sydney wasn't such a bad kid, after all, she just wanted to be heard.

'Anyway, who's up for the best-guided tour ever?' Sydney asked as she marched towards the door.

'Sure.' Rach hurried after her.

'Count me in,' Susie replied.

Remmy and Bridget looked at each other before they eagerly followed the others out of the room. They were all intrigued to see what else Sydney's mansion had to offer. After the tour, they went back to Sydney's bedroom and they all collapsed onto their mattresses. Sydney's house was so huge that they felt tired and overwhelmed. She put a film on her huge TV and they all changed into their PJ's and brushed their teeth.

Remmy hugged her legs close to her as she zoned out, watching the film. Bridget sat down next to her and rested her head on her shoulder.

'Do you think everyone will go to sleep soon?' Bridget yawned.

Remmy peered around her. Sydney was laid out on her bed, painting her nails and occasionally looking up at the film, while Sandy and the vampires were all sitting on Susie's mattress chatting away to each other.

Remmy smiled back. 'I think so.'

'That's good. I'm tired but I don't want to be the first to fall asleep and wake up with ink on my face again.'

'I wouldn't let that happen,' Remmy chuckled.

'I know...but if we both fall asleep first then we'd probably fall victim to their pranks again.' Bridget tried to hide her worry beneath a soft giggle.

'Maybe we should sleep on our fronts,' Remmy suggested.

'I hate doing that, I feel like I can't breathe.'

Remmy laughed. 'Yeah, I know what you mean.'

Both girls were more worried than they were letting on. Remmy knew all too well that Sandy and the vampires were capable of being mean, and Sydney still made her feel uneasy. She didn't want to wake up with chewing gum stuck in her hair or covered in silly string. She tried to push her doubts to one side and to enjoy the sleepover but her fears continued to linger inside her head.

'Does anyone want me to paint their nails?' Sydney held her pot of nail varnish up in the air.

'I'd rather do my own.' Sandy stood up and marched over to the makeup table. 'I love this color.' She picked up a lilac one.

'Fine.' Sydney shrugged. 'Anyone else?'

'You can paint mine.' Rach walked over to her. 'But not that color, I want something that says 'fun' but in a cute way.'

'Sure thing,' Sydney replied.

The door opened and Catherine stepped into the room, a silent Martin behind her. They were both wearing different clothes than they were at dinner. Catherine was now in a tight-fitting blue dress and Martin wore a white striped shirt and perfectly ironed black pants.

'Hey girls, are you all having fun?' Catherine asked.

The girls replied with nods and 'yesses'.

'Great. We'll be popping out for a little bit to see some friends but we won't be too long. No staying up too late.' She wagged a finger at them.

Bridget gave Remmy a horrified look. There was no way her mom would have let her stay if she knew that they'd be left alone at night. Worse still, she couldn't even contact her mother because she didn't have her phone.

'Okay mom,' Sydney replied, as she walked over to the makeup table. 'Have fun.'

Catherine and Martin left the room and an unfazed Sydney searched through her nail varnishes.

'How about dazzling deluxe?' She held up a baby blue shade with silver glitter in it.

'Not cute enough.' Rach stuck up her nose.

'I don't like this,' Bridget whispered to Remmy. 'I want to go home.'

'It's okay, we'll be fine,' Remmy tried to reassure her.

She knew that Janice and Marcus wouldn't have been happy about them being left alone either but she didn't want to worry Bridget any further. Besides, Sydney's parents said they weren't going to be long, so it should all be fine.

'Bridget, are you okay?' Sydney peered over at her.

'Yes, fine,' she muttered.

'Are you sure?' Sydney rose an eyebrow.

'Yeah, I um, how long, um, do you think your parents will be?' Bridget asked.

'Are you scared?' Sandy smirked and the vampires sniggered.

'Shush, Sandy.' Sydney glared at her. 'They will only be a couple of hours. You don't need to worry; this house is like a fort. There are alarms everywhere.'

'I guess so.' Bridget gave a hint of a smile.

'It's going to be an awesome night,' Sydney reassured her.

Chapter Two - The Break-In

All the girls were in their beds chatting with each other. The conversation had turned to school and what they thought of the other students and their teachers. Remmy and Bridget weren't big on gossiping, although so far Sandy and the vampires hadn't been rude about anyone.

'Miss Sutherland is an okay teacher, I guess,' Sydney commented. 'I mean, she's nowhere near as good as my last teacher but she's nice enough and she gave me an A for my last project.'

'Did she? I only got a B+ on that,' Rach grumbled.

'I got an A+,' Sandy smirked.

'Lovely,' Sydney muttered. 'What did you both get?' She looked over at Remmy and Bridget.

'Erm, I got an A,' Remmy replied.

'Same,' Bridget said.

'I got an A too,' Susie added.

'Miss Sutherland's marking system is clearly off. I worked really hard on that stupid project,' Rach huffed.

'It seemed pretty fair to me,' Sandy commented.

'You would say that you got an A+,' Bridget chuckled.

'Maybe she's only allowed to give out so many high marks and by the time she got to yours she'd used them all up,' Susie suggested.

'A B+ is still high,' Remmy said.

'You wouldn't be saying that if you were given it,' Sandy smirked at her.

'Maybe complimenting Miss Sutherland would help you. Last week, I told her that I liked her shoes. I mean, I still would have got a high mark because my project was awesome but if you're nice to her then when she's marking your work, it will stick in her mind. Then she'll like your work more,' Sydney commented.

'That's ridiculous,' Sandy huffed.

'Yeah, Sandy used to be horrible to everyone but she still got high marks,' Bridget replied.

Sandy and the vampires glared at Bridget. Sandy's mouth gaped wide open in disbelief that Bridget would say such a horrible thing about her.

'Sorry.' She blushed before she buried herself further into her sleeping bag.

Remmy tried not to laugh but she couldn't deny that Bridget had a point.

Suddenly, the bedroom light switched off and covered the girls in darkness.

'W-what's going on?' Bridget spluttered.

'It's probably just a blown bulb or something.' Sydney shrugged then hopped out of bed and tried to navigate her way across the room.

'Ouch!' Sandy moaned. 'You just stood on my foot.'

'Sorry,' Sydney chuckled.

'You should know the layout of your own room,' Rach snarled.

'My bedroom doesn't usually have mattresses on the floor.'

She reached the door and flipped the light switch. It didn't work. Then she opened the door to find more darkness.

'The hallway lights are out too.' She flicked the hallway light switch. 'If only Mom hadn't taken our phones, we could have used the flashlights on them.'

'Or used them to phone for help,' Bridget muttered to Remmy.

'It's only a power cut, it's no big deal.' Sandy tried to sound convincing.

'How about we tell each other ghost stories?' Rach suggested.

'Great idea,' Sydney replied.

'I'm really tired,' Sandy said.

'Yeah, same,' Susie agreed.

Remmy and Bridget didn't say anything. The lights going out had freaked them both out and they definitely didn't want to have to listen to ghost stories.

'I understand if you're too scared,' Sydney sniggered.

Sandy faked a yawn. 'I'm not scared, I'm just tired.'

'Yeah, I'm not scared either,' Susie said shakily.

The sound of glass smashing outside caused all the girls to jolt upright.

'What was that?' Sandy asked.

'Relax, it was probably just a cat or something,' Sydney replied.

'Cats don't usually break glass,' Remmy whispered.

They all fell silent and looked at each other's dark outlines. Remmy put her hand over her chest. She could feel her heart pounding. Bridget gulped, she wanted to bury herself back in her sleeping bag but she was too afraid to move.

The front door opened and then closed with a BANG! Footsteps echoed through the downstairs of the house.

'Call the police,' Bridget whispered to Sydney.

'We haven't got our phones, remember,' Remmy whispered back.

'Where's the house phone?' Bridget asked, her voice was on the verge of becoming hysterical.

'Downstairs, near the front door.'

'What are we going to do?' Sandy hissed.

'Nothing. It's probably just my parents,' Sydney said.

'If it was your parents then why did the lights go out and glass smash?'

'It's nothing. Look, I'll go downstairs and see what's going on.'

Sydney walked over to the door and put her hand on the doorknob. She paused there as she heard scraping sounds downstairs, which sounded like the furniture being moved. Remmy and Bridget huddled together and held each other's hands. Both girls were shaking uncontrollably.

'Where can we hide?' Susie whispered. Fear could be heard

in her shaky voice.

Sydney gestured them over to her walk-in-wardrobe and opened the doors. The other girls crept over to it, their eyes now adjusted to the dark. They all knelt down in the wardrobe. Sydney quietly closed the doors before she covered them in clothes. They sat there in as much silence as they could manage. Bridget and Susie were both silently crying, Rach's breathing was frantic and Remmy's heart rate grew even faster.

After twenty minutes had passed they realized that Sydney's parents weren't coming to rescue them.

'We need to get to the house phone and call the police,' Sandy whispered.

'I'll go,' Sydney said.

'No.' Remmy grabbed her hand. 'You can't go out there, it's too dangerous.'

'It's okay, I'll hide if I hear or see anyone.'

Sydney slowly got up and opened the door as quietly as she could. She gave the girls a nervous wave before she closed the doors behind her. Bridget stood up and Remmy immediately grabbed her wrist.

'What are you doing?' Remmy whispered.

'I can't let Syd go by herself, so I'm going with her.'

'No.' Remmy refused to let go of her arm. 'You don't know the layout of the house. You'll probably end up knocking something over in the dark and then you'll both be seen.'

Bridget sighed and then crouched back down next to Remmy. They huddled their shaking bodies together. Susie was sobbing onto the shoulder of Sandy's t-shirt and Rach had a firm grip on Sandy's arm. Was this it? Were they going to die, terrified in Sydney's large but stuffy wardrobe? Would they never get to see their families again? Remmy pictured her mom's warm face. This couldn't be it, she needed to see her again. She needed to see Charlie again, she needed to have her very first kiss. None of them could die here, not like this!

Five minutes passed. Five minutes of agonizing waiting. Was Sydney okay? Had she made it to the phone? Where was she now?

A single, high-pitched scream echoed through the house. All the girls looked at each other before huddling in closer together. They were each crying silent tears as they shook violently. Remmy clamped her teeth down hard to try and quieten her frantic breathing.

They heard the bedroom door swing open. Footsteps crossed the room. A beam of light shone through the gap in the wardrobe like a laser. Someone was out there. They weren't alone!

They didn't know what to do, fear had paralyzed them. They all looked at each other through tear-stained eyes, convinced that they were about to die.

The footsteps grew closer and closer. The beam of light intensified. Sandy and Rach gripped tightly onto each other's arms and Susie kept her face buried into Sandy's shoulder.

Someone was out there. Whoever it was had Sydney and now they were coming for them.

They heard heavy breathing lingering directly outside the wardrobe. They all held their breath and froze like statues.

The wardrobe doors swung open. Their eyes adjusted to the bright light. Three figures stood in front of them, they were all dressed in black tops with the hoods pulled up over their heads. They all had blood-stained hands, the front person was holding a torch in one hand and a blood-covered knife in the other.

All of the girls screamed...each of them was convinced that this was the end.

The figures took a step towards them. The girls ducked down.

'Surprise!!!' the three figures shouted.

The three people pulled down their hoods and grinned widely. It took the girls a moment to realize what was happening. Standing in front of them were Catherine, Martin, and Sydney. Remmy stared at them open-mouthed as she took in the plastic knife in Sydney's fake-blood covered hand.

All three began to laugh but the girls continued to stare back in disbelief. Sandy pulled the layer of clothes off and trudged out of the wardrobe. Remmy's heart was still in overdrive and she wondered if it would ever slow down.

'Got ya!' Sydney sniggered. 'You should have seen your faces.'

'It's got you,' Catherine corrected her. 'But your faces were a picture.'

'I-I d-don't understand,' Rach spluttered out.

'Well, Sydney told us that you girls love a prank. This was all her idea.' Catherine ruffled her hand through her hair.

'B-but, why?' Sandy asked.

Sydney shrugged. 'Relax, it was only a bit of fun. No big deal.'

'Anyway, we'll leave you girls to it.' Catherine and Martin headed towards the door.

Catherine switched the light on and the girls blinked as they adjusted their eyes to the brightness.

'No more practical jokes, we promise.' Martin's lips curled slightly at the sides. The girls weren't sure if he was smiling or being serious.

Remmy and Bridget slumped down onto the couch. They were both still in shock and were incapable of words. Neither of them had ever been so scared before and they never wanted to go through anything like that ever again. Rach looked down at her aching arm, she had red marks where Sandy had gripped onto it. She rubbed it as she glared at Sydney.

Sandy grabbed the pillow off her mattress, walked over to Sydney and began hitting her with it. Sydney let her have the first couple of hits before she grabbed a pillow off her bed and began to hit Sandy back. Sandy and Sydney both began to laugh as they carried on their pillow fight. Rach and Susie grabbed their pillows and joined in. Remmy and Bridget stayed where they were and watched. They were both still shaken up and definitely not in the mood for a pillow fight.

'I want to go home,' Bridget whispered to Remmy.

'Me too,' Remmy whispered back.

Eventually, they all grew tired and flopped down onto their mattresses.

'That was the worst, yet at the same time the best prank ever!' Rach said.

'Yeah, I was totally freaked out,' Susie giggled.

'Me too. Especially the part when you went downstairs and screamed.'

'The part where you heavy-breathed outside the wardrobe was the worst!' Sandy exclaimed. 'I thought we were all going to be killed by some madman!'

Rach shook her head. 'I can't believe you concocted the whole thing.'

'Well, I did,' Sydney smirked. 'And I totally sucked all of you in!'

'You should be a film writer or something,' Susie remarked.

'I suppose it could be a career option if my modeling dreams don't pay off.'

'Remmy, which bit scared you the most?' Sandy asked.

Remmy didn't want to answer. She was still in shock and felt upset by what had happened. The other girls may have found it funny but she didn't.

'The last bit,' she muttered.

'I made my mom take me to the fancy dress shop for the fake blood and the plastic knife, and we ordered the hoodies online.'

'So, you've been planning this all week?' Sandy asked, shaking her head.

'Yep. It's been fun planning it all. We had a few practices to get the timing right but it went far better than I ever could have imagined.'

'You got me...but can there be no more pranks tonight?' Susie pleaded.

'Sure,' Sydney grinned. 'I wouldn't do any more tonight anyway. I could never manage to top that one.'

'Good, I don't want to have to sleep with one eye open,' Rach giggled.

Susie yawned. 'Your prank has tired me out.'

'Me too,' Sydney smirked. 'I'm going to have a wash; I'm still covered in fake blood.'

Sydney walked into the bathroom, leaving the other girls by themselves. Sandy and the vampires all exchanged looks. They'd been shaken up by Sydney's prank but now they could see the funny side.

Sandy looked at the vampires. 'She'd better not pull any more pranks, that one has totally drained me.'

'Yeah, it was intense,' Rach said.

Sandy grinned. 'We'll get her back.'

'We SO have to,' Rach replied.

'Yes, we so do,' Susie added.

Remmy looked at Bridget, she was curled up on her mattress. She could tell that she was still shaking because her bedcover was moving.

'Bridge, are you okay?' she whispered to her.

'Fine,' Bridget squeaked back.

Sydney came back from the bathroom and got into bed. The girls chatted with each other for a bit before they fell silent and tried to fall asleep. Remmy could hear the sounds of Bridget softly crying to herself, so she leaned over and wrapped her arm around her. One by one, the girls fell asleep until Bridget was the last one awake. She couldn't bear to close her eyes because when she did, she heard the shattering of glass, Sydney's high pitched scream and saw the three hooded figures.

The darkness had shifted into the light of early morning and birds were chirping outside when Bridget's tiredness won out and she finally fell asleep.

Chapter Three - The Next Morning

Remmy was the first to wake-up. She didn't want to disturb the other girls so she looked up at the ceiling and replayed the events of the night in her head. It didn't surprise her that Sydney had come up with such an elaborate plan to make her sleepover unforgettable. There was no way that her mom and Marcus would have ever agreed to take part in something so mean. This wasn't a normal way for parents to act, but then again Sydney's parents seemed far from normal. Having an alarm on their fridge was seriously weird. She didn't understand why they had it. It was obvious they weren't struggling for lack of money or food. She thought back to finding Sydney vomiting in the bathroom. She'd been adamant that Remmy shouldn't tell anyone...but why did she want to keep her vomiting fit a secret?

She'd read in a Girlfriend magazine that some girls and boys had eating disorders because they disliked the way they looked. When they looked in the mirror they saw a different person looking back, one that they judged to be unattractive. It didn't matter how slim or pretty they were, they'd never see it. Was Sydney one of those girls? Was she making herself vomit because she feared that if she put weight on then she wouldn't be her mom's idea of perfect anymore? Was the alarm on the fridge to stop Sydney from eating more than what her mom thought was acceptable?

One thing was for sure, this was a weird family and she didn't want to be in this house anymore. She wanted to go home to her unconventional, slightly crazy family. At least they didn't have an alarm on the fridge or carry out cruel pranks on her friends.

Catherine barged into the room and clapped her hands together. 'Wake-up girls, breakfast will be ready in fifteen minutes.' She smiled at them before walking out of the room.

Sandy darted out of bed, grabbed her bag and then raced into the bathroom.

'Morning,' Remmy said to a groggy looking Bridget. 'Did you sleep okay?'

'Eventually,' Bridget muttered.

'We'll be going home soon.'

Bridget managed a smile back. The thought of going home was the best part of this whole trip. There was no way she was ever coming to Sydney's for a sleepover again. In fact, she wasn't sure if she ever wanted to go to a sleepover at *anyone's* house ever again.

'I'd hurry up if I were you, my mom doesn't like to be kept waiting,' Sydney said, as she hopped out of bed.

Remmy and Bridget exchanged looks before they both crawled out of bed and rifled through their bags. Sandy came out of the bathroom and Sydney hurried into it. She was surprisingly quick for Sydney. Soon, all the girls were dressed and had used the bathroom. They all followed Sydney downstairs. Sandy and the vampires were excited to see what was for breakfast, while Remmy lingered behind them alongside Bridget, who had barely said anything.

They walked into the large, dazzling white kitchen, expecting to see the chef cooking for them. To their surprise, Catherine was gripping hold of a frying pan on top of the gas stove.

'Hi, girls." She waved them in. 'I'm cooking buckwheat pancakes and you'll have them with fresh fruit.'

Sandy exchanged confused looks with the rest of the vampires. None of them had any idea what buckwheat was. Still, they all followed Sydney over to the table and sat down. Catherine walked over and began to serve the pancakes.

'I don't believe in using white flour, it's bad for you. I don't use cream or ice cream either, way too much sugar. But there's some ricotta cheese instead.' She gestured to a bowl filled with a white-looking concoction in the middle of the table.

They all took a reluctant bite and were pleasantly surprised. They weren't as good as the pancakes that they had at home but they weren't bad. Remmy loaded her pancake up with fresh fruit and dabbed a small spoonful of ricotta cheese onto it. She put a forkful into her mouth and chewed on it. That's when she noticed Bridget was twirling a strawberry around on her fork...her pancakes untouched.

'Are you okay?' she whispered to her.

'Yeah, I'm just not feeling very hungry.' Bridget forced a smile.

Catherine commented, 'I don't know why people feel the need to eat so unhealthily when the healthy versions taste so much better. After all, we are what we eat.' She looked straight at Sydney as she said this and then smiled at the others. 'Would you girls like some more?'

'Yes please,' Sandy smiled back at her. 'They're delicious.'

Rach and Susie also eagerly asked for more.

Catherine nodded before she placed another pancake onto

each of their plates.

'What about you two?' She looked at Remmy and Bridget. 'Oh! Is something wrong?' She looked down at Bridget's barely touched food.

'No, nothing.' Bridget blushed. 'I'm just not feeling that hungry.'

'Can I have another one please?' Remmy tried to take the attention away from Bridget.

'Of course.' Catherine used the spatula in her hand to transfer a pancake onto Remmy's plate.

Sydney was hungrily eyeing the plate of extra pancakes. Her mom noticed and gave her a stern look.

'I'm going to the bathroom,' Sydney muttered.

Remmy watched her leave the room and wondered if she was going to the bathroom to make herself sick again. She didn't know if she should go and check on Sydney or not. She didn't want to accuse someone of having an eating disorder when she wasn't sure.

There were pancakes left over but Catherine didn't offer any more to the girls. Sandy and the vampires licked their lips as they eyed them but they weren't willing to take any without being offered first. Catherine took Sydney's plate away and loaded it into the dishwasher. Sandy and Rach looked at the leftover pancakes and then at each other. But then Catherine walked back over to the table, so they both directed their gaze at their plates.

Sydney walked back into the room just as the intercom sounded and Rach's dad spoke into it.

'You girls had better go and pack,' Catherine said before she

42

headed towards the door.

They all rushed upstairs and packed their bags. Sydney sat on her bed and swung out her legs as she watched her friends.

'Thanks for coming, it's been so much fun,' she grinned. 'But, maybe it's best if you don't tell your parents about the prank. You know what adults can be like, they take everything so seriously.'

'That's fine, I won't tell,' Sandy replied.

'Yeah same,' Rach said.

'Sure,' Susie agreed.

Remmy and Bridget exchanged worried looks.

'Girls, is there something wrong?' Sydney looked at them.

'I don't lie to my parents,' Bridget muttered.

'It's not lying if you don't tell them. Besides, what happens in my house, stays in my house,' Sydney scoffed.

'I guess.' Bridget stared down at her bag.

'Remmy?' Sydney looked at her.

'Yeah, I won't say anything.'

'Great!' Sydney smiled at them encouragingly. 'I've had such a good time, you'll all have to come and stay again soon!'

Bridget coughed and then gave Remmy an alarmed look. They all grabbed their bags and followed Sydney down the spiral staircase and into the kitchen where their parents were talking to Catherine as they sipped from their cups of herbal tea. When Bridget saw her mom, she instantly dropped her bag onto the floor, ran over and wrapped her arms around her. Her mom was so taken by surprise that she only just managed not to spill her drink.

'I've missed you,' Bridget mumbled into her mom's blouse.

'Aw honey, I've missed you too. You had a good time though, didn't you?'

'Yeah.'

Catherine placed a box containing the girls' phones down on the table. 'Here you go, girls.'

The girls all dropped their bags and rushed over to grab their phones. Some of the parents gave Catherine a confused look.

'I wanted them to have fun without all this technology...like it was back in our day.'

'I see,' Marcus muttered.

'I'm surprised you managed to convince Rach to hand her phone over, she's usually glued to it,' Rach's mom chuckled.

'They were happy to co-operate. They are all lovely girls and they're welcome here anytime.'

Remmy and Bridget swapped looks of dread.

'We'd better get going. Thank you very much for having Remmy and Sandy,' Janice said.

Sandy gave a sickly-sweet smile. 'Thank you for having me,'

'Thank you.' Remmy forced a smile as well.

Catherine beamed. 'You're all very welcome.'

The other parents and girls said their goodbyes before

walking out of the house and over to their cars. Catherine and Sydney waved from the doorway. Marcus piled the girls' bags into the trunk then he took a step back and looked up at the house enviously.

'One day...' he whispered to Janice.

'No, thank you. All our spare time would be taken up with cleaning,' she laughed.

He leaned over and kissed her on the cheek before they both got into the car. Remmy looked over at Sandy, who was waving at her friends through the car window. Sandy didn't seem to be affected by Sydney's prank, whereas Remmy couldn't get it out of her head. She thought about poor Bridget sobbing herself to sleep. That wasn't right, sleepovers were meant to be fun...not make you fear for your life. She wanted to talk to Sandy about whether they should tell Janice and Marcus, but she knew she'd have to wait until later and speak to her alone.

They all waved at Sydney and her mom as Marcus drove off down the street.

'Did you have a lovely time?' Janice turned her head to look at them.

'It was amazing; her house is a mansion! Everything is expensive and there's so much gold everywhere. They even had gold-leaf wallpaper. And they have a maid and a chef and they've got an alarm on their fridge.' The words spilled out of Sandy's mouth.

'An alarm, whatever for?' Janice raised an eyebrow and looked completely puzzled.

'Because Sydney used to be really fat and her mom doesn't want her sneaking extra food.'

'Oh right,' Janice gave a flustered look. 'Remmy, did you have a good time?'

'Yeah, great.' Remmy's voice sounded totally flat.

'We had buckwheat pancakes for breakfast because Catherine doesn't believe in unhealthy foods. They were weird but in a good way, although your pancakes are way better,' Sandy prattled on.

'The herbal tea she gave us was interesting, wasn't it Marcus?' Catherine smiled.

'Yes, you could say that,' he replied.

'I'm glad you both had a good time. We'll have to ask Sydney to stay over soon,' Janice suggested.

Both girls fell silent. Sandy had enjoyed visiting Sydney's house but she didn't trust the girl and she didn't particularly like her. There was no way she wanted her snooping through her belongings and judging her.

As for Remmy, right now, she never wanted to see Sydney ever again. Her prank was terrifying and her entire family was strange. She'd also traumatized Bridget, which was cruel and unnecessary.

The rest of the journey was mostly in silence. When their house came into view, Remmy gave a sigh of relief. It definitely felt good to be home.

Chapter Four – Still Shattered

Remmy was sitting cross-legged on Sandy's bed, chewing on her nails. Sandy sat opposite her but her main focus was directed at her phone. A Taylor Swift song was blasting out of her laptop and she was nodding her head in time to it.

'So, that was a crazy sleepover,' Remmy said.

'Yeah, I guess.' Sandy kept her attention on her phone.

'Sydney's parents were…intense.'

'Yeah, they seem odd but then again...Sydney's odd too.'

'Yes she is.' Remmy sighed. 'Look, I think we should tell my mom and Marcus about the prank.'

'No!' Sandy looked up from her phone. 'No way!!! If you tell them then they'll never let us go anywhere until we're at least twenty-one. Is that what you want?'

'No.' Remmy shook her head.

'Then you have to keep quiet.'

Remmy nodded. She agreed with Sandy. Telling Janice and Marcus would probably result in them never being allowed to go to any more sleepovers ever again. Although after the experience she'd just had, she was perfectly happy with staying at home. And she didn't want Sandy to be mad at her, as she definitely didn't need her turning back into 'bully' Sandy.

'You're doing the right thing.' Sandy leaned over and patted Remmy's hand.

'I'm never going to another sleepover at Sydney's house again.'

'You don't have to,' Sandy smiled. 'Look, I know that Sydney and her family are super weird but it was just a prank. Okay, so maybe they took it a bit too far but it's not their fault that Bridget is so sensitive.'

Remmy nodded again. She didn't want to tell Sandy just how much the prank had upset her too. She was pretty sure that she'd be having nightmares about it for weeks and that she'd definitely need to sleep with the light on.

'Are you coming out to the pool?' Sandy asked. 'I want to work on my tan.'

'Yeah, I guess. I'm just going to do a few things first,' Remmy smiled half-heartedly.

'Okay then.' Sandy returned her attention to her phone.

Remmy got up off Sandy's bed and gave her a wave (that she didn't notice) left the room and walked into her own. She slumped down onto her bed, thoughts of the prank circling in her head. Not telling her mom about it didn't sit easily in her stomach. She pulled her laptop off her side table and lifted the lid. If only Amelia was on FB so she could message her. She always offered the best advice. Remmy switched her laptop on and then chewed on some gum as she watched the screen load. She had no way of contacting Amelia, so right now she was on her own.

She logged into FB and sent Bridget a message:

>Hey Bridget…just checking that you're okay?

She sat back and waited for a reply…but one didn't come. Deciding that she couldn't stay in her room to be harassed by her thoughts, she changed into her navy-blue swimming costume and headed out to the pool. As she walked outside, she smelled burning charcoal and there was a cloud of smoke surrounding Marcus.

'Hi, Remmy.' Janice was sitting at the outside table. 'It's such a lovely day, we decided to have a barbecue.'

'Great.' Remmy forced a tight smile and watched as Sandy helped Janice set out plates on the table.

'I'll go and get some juice,' Remmy offered.

'Thank you, sweetheart.'

Remmy walked into the kitchen and grabbed the juice bottle. She carried it outside and placed it on the table.

'Thank you, girls, I can finish up here,' Janice smiled at them.

They both lay down on sunbeds by the pool and Sandy put her large sunglasses on and her headphones in her ears. Remmy looked at her, she seemed so relaxed...whereas Remmy felt anything but relaxed. A breeze caused a door inside to slam shut and Remmy jumped with such a start that she almost fell off her sunbed. She peered around her before laying back down on it. She tapped her fingers against the side of the sunbed and fought back tears. She couldn't relax, she was in a constant panic that a hooded figure would come charging out of the kitchen with a blood-covered knife.

When the food was ready they all sat around the pool to eat it.

'So, girls, did anything interesting happen at the sleepover?' Janice asked.

Remmy was so alarmed by this question that she swallowed

her piece of steak the wrong way. She found herself choking, and as hard as she tried she couldn't breathe properly. Marcus hurried over to her and hit her on the back. The piece of steak shot out of her mouth and landed in front of Sandy.

'Gross! Did you have to spit it at me?' Sandy barked at her.

'Thanks!' Remmy blushed as she looked at Marcus.

'That's quite alright.' He gave an awkward smile before he walked back over to his seat.

'Sweetheart, are you okay?' Her mom passed her a glass of water.

'Yes thanks,' Remmy croaked, turning an even deeper shade of red as she took the glass.

'The sleepover was great, we played truth and dare and watched a movie. So yeah, normal girl stuff really,' Sandy said with ease.

Remmy sipped on her water. Telling lies was easy for Sandy but it didn't come as naturally to her.

'This is so good.' Sandy lifted up her burger. 'Sydney's mom is such a health freak, we had asparagus wrapped in parma ham for our starter and she served the buckwheat pancakes with ricotta cheese. I mean, it was okay but it had nothing on your pancakes, Janice.' She took a big bite of her steak burger.

'Ricotta cheese, how different,' Janice remarked.

'Yes. But please don't start using it, I'd much prefer cream.'

Janice laughed. 'I wasn't planning to, but maybe I should give it a try.'

'No way!' Sandy shook her head.

'Don't worry, I'm only joking.'

'Good, I love your pancakes,' Sandy smiled at her.

Remmy looked over at Sandy, she was super confident and good at diversion. If Sandy hadn't managed to divert the conversation, Remmy would definitely have ended up blurting out the news of Sydney's prank. She was worried that her mom would ask her something else about the sleepover, so she wolfed down the remainder of her lunch and then stood up.

'Thanks for lunch but it's so hot out here.' She fanned herself with her hand. 'And I have an assignment to finish.'

'Okay, Remmy.' Janice nodded. 'I take it you girls didn't get much sleep. Were you too busy chatting and watching movies?'

'Something like that,' Remmy muttered.

'We did stay up quite late as we were talking,' Sandy quickly added.

Remmy took this opportunity to hurry back into the house before her mom could ask her any more questions. She didn't like deceiving her mom but she didn't want to fall out with Sandy either. She said that she wouldn't tell, so the easiest way for her to stick to this was by avoiding her mom as much as possible for the rest of the day.

She closed her bedroom door then walked over to her curtains and closed them too. She wanted to block the sun out so she wasn't reminded of the warm sunny day that she was missing out on. She wanted to close herself off from the world.

Ding!

She looked down at her open laptop and saw that she was still logged into her FB page and that Bridget had replied.

>*Sorry for the slow reply, I fell asleep as soon as I got home. I'm still a bit shaky but I'm okay. Have you told your mom what happened?*

>No. Sandy thinks that if we tell her then we won't be allowed out until we're old. Have you told your mom?

>*No. But part of me wants to. I won't for now but I'll have to stay in my room. I'm worried that I'll blurt it out to her.*

>Bridget! That's what I'm doing too…hiding in my room!

>*I won't say anything for now but I'm never staying at Sydney's ever again!!!!!*

>Me too. That prank was horrible!

>*I know. Every time I close my eyes I see them standing there in those hoodies and I see that knife!*

>Same. We're home now though.

>*I'm so happy I'm home. Anyway, I'm still shattered so I'm going back to sleep. I'll see you at school. x*

>I'm glad you're okay. See you tomorrow. x

Remmy placed her laptop down on her bedside table and then fell back onto her bed. It was so hot and stuffy and she longed to be sitting back outside by the pool. She sighed to herself as she looked up at the ceiling.

'Bridget's okay. I'm okay. It's over with now, so it's all okay,' she told herself out loud, but she found herself struggling to believe her own words.

Chapter Five - Bridget's Got a BF

Monday morning arrived and Marcus dropped Remmy and Sandy off at school. Both of them waved to Marcus before walking away.

Sandy yawned. 'School sucks. There should be a three-day weekend.'

'Yeah.' Remmy stared down at her sneakers.

'Remmy!' Bridget shouted from behind them.

Both girls turned around and smiled at Bridget.

'Hey Bridge,' Remmy said.

'Hey.'

'Have you recovered from the weekend?' Sandy smirked.

Bridget blushed. 'Yeah.'

They all walked over to Rach and Susie who were standing near the entrance. They greeted each other with a mixture of hugs and awkward smiles.

'How amazing was Sydney's sleepover?' Sandy grinned.

'Yeah, it was awesome,' Rach replied.

'Her house is incredible,' Susie said.

Sandy chuckled.

'And that prank was so funny,' Sandy chuckled.

'Yeah, it was great, she totally got me,' Rach giggled in

agreement.

'Yeah, me too,' said Susie.

Remmy and Bridget both stared at their feet. They didn't want to talk about the prank, they didn't want to talk about the sleepover at all. They were both trying to forget that it had ever happened.

Sandy smirked at them. 'You're both being very quiet.'

'Hey, guys!' Sydney waved as she walked towards them. 'So, girlfriends, what are you talking about?'

'We were raving about how AMAZING your house and sleepover were,' Rach replied.

'I know, right?'

'Bridget, didn't you enjoy the sleepover?' Sandy asked her.

Bridget's cheeks flamed as red as her hair. She gave Remmy an awkward look as she tried to think of a reply. 'I guess I enjoyed some of it but I wasn't so keen on the break-in prank.'

'Don't be such a cry-baby.' Sydney flicked her hair behind her back.

'Yeah Bridget, it was just a bit of fun,' Sandy sniggered.

The rest of the vampires laughed and Rach mocked Bridget by sucking on her thumb.

'Stop it!' Remmy said sternly. 'The prank was definitely something to remember but I didn't like it either.'

Bridget smiled gratefully at her friend. They were both thankful that they had each other's backs.

'Cry-babies.' Sydney frowned at them. 'If you can't take a little prank then you really are both ridiculous.'

'Yeah, it was only a joke, don't be so totally pathetic,' Rach scoffed.

'It didn't bother us!' Susie remarked.

Remmy recalled how upset and frightened Susie had looked when she was crouched in Sydney's wardrobe. She thought about bringing this up but decided against it.

'Well, it upset us. It was cruel and not at all funny,' Remmy countered.

'Whatever.' Sydney rolled her eyes. 'Let's get away from the cry-babies.' She gestured for the others to follow her.

They all stuck their noses up at Remmy and Bridget as they walked away from them and followed Sydney into the school building.

Remmy looked at Bridget. 'Ignore them.'

Bridget nodded. 'It looks like the vampires have gained a new member.'

Remmy was about to reply when she saw Colin heading towards them. Bridget instantly brightened up, a wide smile appearing on her face.

He waved at the two girls 'Hi, Bridget. Hi Remmy. How goes it?'

'Good.' Bridget blushed. 'You?'

'All the better for seeing you.'

Remmy smiled to herself, she liked seeing her friends happy.

'So, I guess we'd better start heading to class,' Bridget said.

'Yep, we don't want Miss Sutherland freaking out at us.' He chuckled. 'Her eyes are so round when she gets mad, they look like Frisbees,'

Bridget laughed shyly as she walked alongside him.

'So, Bridge, I was wondering, um, if you wanted to um, hang out after school?' Colin asked.

There was a brief pause as both Colin and Remmy looked at the blushing Bridget.

'Yeah, cool. I mean, sure. Sure, I'd like that,' Bridget smiled at him.

He grinned back. 'Great.'

'Remmy and Charlie should come too, it can be like a double date.' She clasped her hands over her mouth. 'I didn't mean to say a date, I meant hang-out or meet-up, or um, yeah. Not date.'

Colin placed his hand on Bridget's arm and looked her straight in the eyes. 'A double date sounds good to me.'

Bridget coughed and then blushed even more so that her cheeks were a brilliant red. She couldn't muster a reply so she smiled at him.

'A double date it is then,' Remmy grinned. 'Charlie and I were going to meet on the boardwalk for a milkshake at four o'clock, so that sounds perfect.'

She was excited for her friends, as she knew how much they liked each other and how much they deserved to be happy. She also couldn't wait to tell Charlie about their double date. Bridget and Colin continued to give each other lovey-dovey looks as they walked into class. Miss Sutherland wasn't there yet so Remmy rushed over to Charlie's desk.

'Hey, Remmy.' He gave her a huge smile.

She beamed at him. 'Guess what?'

He grinned. 'You've been voted the world's cutest girlfriend?'

'Please...' Sandy brought her fingers up to her mouth and made gagging sounds.

'Nope.' Remmy ignored Sandy and lowered her voice as she whispered to Charlie. 'We're going on a double date with Bridget and Colin.'

'He finally got the courage to ask her?' he replied quietly.

'Yep!'

'It took him long enough; he's had a crush on her all year.'

'It's so exciting.' Remmy kept her voice low.

'I'm impressed he finally worked up the confidence to ask her out.'

'What are you two whispering about?' Sandy glared at them.

Charlie smirked at her. 'None of your business.'

'Whatever.' Sandy folded her arms and turned her head away from them.

Miss Sutherland walked into the room with her arms full of books.

'See you at break time,' Remmy smiled at Charlie before heading to her desk.

She placed her backpack down on her desk and sat down. As she was rummaging through it to look for her pencil case, Sydney sniggered at her. At first, Remmy ignored her but then Sydney sniggered again.

'What is it?' Remmy looked up at Sydney.

'I was just wondering if you were looking for your pacifier or your teddy bear?'

Remmy gave her a confused frown then shook her head and went back to searching through her bag.

'Because you're such a cry-baby and all,' Sydney added.

Remmy chewed on the side of her lip. She thought about Amelia and what she would say about the situation.

She held her head up high and turned to look at Sydney. 'I must have left them at home.'

Sydney rolled her eyes before feigning interest in her notebook. Remmy placed her backpack underneath her desk and then looked over at Bridget. Sydney's petty comments had no effect on her good mood because she was so happy that Bridget and Colin were going on a date.

Bridget excitedly tapped her fingers against her desk. Miss Sutherland was talking but she couldn't concentrate on a word she said...all she could think about was Colin and their date. It was a date, wasn't it? Or had he just meant to ask her out as friends? She knew that she liked him but what if he didn't like her like that? What if she spilled milkshake all over herself? What if he didn't turn up? What would her mother think? She found that her excitement had turned into worry. There were so many things that could go wrong. She'd never been on a date before and she didn't know how she was meant to act.

She tried to shake the bad thoughts out of her head. This date was happening because Colin was a really nice boy. He actually did like her and she liked him too. It would be fine, everything would be fine. She just had to be herself and it would be amazing, wouldn't it?

'It'll be great,' she told herself. 'Just be yourself.'

What if being herself wasn't good enough? What if she did something embarrassing like falling over or saying something stupid? What if Colin thought they were going on a friendship date and she'd imagined that it was something more?

'Just breathe,' she told herself. 'It'll be fine, completely fine.'

***

School passed by slowly and Bridget found her excitement growing and also her nerves. She arrived at the boardwalk early and hopped from one foot to the other as she waited for the others to arrive.

When she saw Remmy walking towards her, she spluttered, 'Remmy, what if Colin doesn't turn up?'

'Bridget, he's mad about you. Of course, he's going to turn up.'

'I hope so!'

'Look!' Remmy pointed across the road to where Charlie and Colin were standing.

'Oh no, oh no, oh no.' Bridget waved her hands in front of her face. 'I don't know how to act on a date. I don't know what to do.'

'Just be you.' Remmy gave her a reassuring smile.

'Okay.' Bridget took a deep breath.

'Honestly Bridge, Colin's crazy about you.'

'You think?'

'I know.'

The boys crossed the road and walked towards the girls. Remmy gave Charlie a wave and a smile whilst Colin couldn't take his eyes off Bridget.

Bridget found herself relaxing and she couldn't stop smiling as Colin approached her.

'Hey girls, you're looking as beautiful as ever.' Colin continued to stare at Bridget as he spoke.

Bridget blushed and gave him an awkward smile.

'Milkshakes await.' Charlie took Remmy's hand.

They walked along the boardwalk. Remmy's fingers tingled beneath Charlie's. She was so happy to be his girlfriend and she was excited for her friends. She had a large smile on her face as she walked towards the cafe.

They sat in a booth by the window and ordered milkshakes and a huge bowl of fries to share. Bridget and Colin were sitting next to each other and they kept on giving each other lovey-dovey glances.

'We should do this again,' Remmy said as she slurped through her straw.

'Yes, we should,' Charlie grinned at her. 'I'm down for this double dating.'

Bridget turned bright red and Colin almost choked on his milkshake.

He looked at Bridget. 'Would you, um, like that? I mean, um, to go on another um, date?'

'Yes,' she said eagerly. Not wanting to appear too eager, she added, 'I mean, cool. I'd like that.'

'Cool.'

'Yes, it's cool,' Charlie chuckled.

Colin grinned. 'I'm a cool guy.'

'And Bridget's a cool girl,' Remmy said.

'That she is.' Colin gave her a soppy look.

'So, where next?' Remmy asked. 'Are we going for a walk along the boardwalk?'

'Sounds good to me,' Charlie grinned.

Bridget blushed. 'Me too.'

'And me,' Colin said.

'Great, I'll go and ask for the bill.' Charlie jumped out of his seat.

Bridget took her purple purse out of her backpack.

'I'll get this.' Colin said.

'You don't have to do that.' Bridget shook her head.

'Bridget, it's just a shake. Besides, I want to.' Colin gave her a toothy smile.

She smiled shyly. 'Thanks, Colin.'

Remmy couldn't hide her own smile. They were so cute together.

Charlie came back with the bill. Digging deep into his pocket, he pulled out a crinkled ten-dollar bill.

Remmy placed a ten-dollar bill of her own down on the table and looked at Charlie. 'You got the last one, so it's my turn.'

'Are you sure?' Charlie asked.

'Yep, I can treat my boyfriend to a milkshake.'

'You're the best girlfriend ever.' Charlie reached for Remmy's hand.

'Pass me the sick bucket,' Colin chuckled.

Charlie grinned back. 'Like you can talk.'

Bridget blushed as she looked down at the table. She really

liked Colin and their date had gone really well. She wanted to be his girlfriend so badly but she wanted him to ask her. A boy had never asked her out before and she was both excited and terrified at the prospect of it. She had no idea how her mom would respond to her having a boyfriend but she was pretty sure that she would like Colin. He was so kind and funny and easy to talk to. He liked her! A cute boy actually liked her!!!

They were walking out of the cafe just as the doors swung open and Sandy, the vampires and Sydney walked in.

'Hi, Charlie.' Sydney pouted at him, completely ignoring the others.

'Hey,' he smiled.

'There's a funny smell in here.' Sydney wafted her hand in front of her face and the vampires all sniggered.

'It smells fine to me,' Charlie said obliviously.

'Too many cry-babies around for my liking,' Sydney said under her breath.

'Huh?' Charlie gave Sydney a confused look.

'It doesn't matter.' Sydney touched his shoulder and smiled. 'See you later Charlie.'

Remmy frowned as she watched Sydney lead the vampires over to a table. Sandy looked back at her and shrugged before she hurried after the others. Bridget looked uncomfortable as she looked down at the floor.

'What was that about?' Charlie asked.

'No idea,' Remmy replied.

'That girl is weird,' Colin commented.

Charlie smiled. 'Nah, she's okay.'

Remmy tried to hide her frown. She didn't think Sydney was okay at all. Instead, she thought that she was cruel and hurtful. Okay, so they hadn't liked her prank, it didn't mean that they deserved to be teased for it. She decided that Bridget was right, it definitely seemed as though the vampires had a new member.

They left the café and walked along the boardwalk. Remmy and Charlie walked further ahead to give Bridget and Colin some space, but Remmy couldn't resist peering back at them.

'Remmy, come on.' Charlie gently pulled on her arm and grinned. 'Give the lovebirds some privacy.'

'Okay, it's just so hard not to watch them, they look so happy.'

He took her hand and pressed it. 'Yeah, I know that feeling.' He looked straight at her.

They smiled at each other and Remmy felt her heart hammering in her chest.

'Come on, let's walk ahead,' Charlie insisted.

They continued onwards, swinging their hands as they moved. Bridget watched them. She had always been happy for her friends but at the same time, there had been a part of her that yearned to have what they had. She had been convinced that no boy would ever like her in that way...but Colin liked her and she liked him.

'Want to sit for a minute?' Colin pointed over to the wall.

Bridget nodded. 'Okay.'

Colin smiled at her. 'Thanks for coming out with me.'

'Thanks for the milkshake. I've had a great time.' Bridget nervously tapped her fingers against the wall.

'Me too.' Colin gently placed his hand on top of Bridget's. 'You don't need to fidget.'

She blushed and smiled at him. 'Sorry.'

'Don't be sorry, I like it. I like you.'

'I like you too.' She blushed even harder.

'Bridget, I um. There's um, there's something I um, I want to um, ask you,' he muttered nervously.

'Yes?' she looked at him.

'I was wondering if you would, um, if you'd like to be my girlfriend?'

She looked into his eyes, double-checking that he wasn't joking.

'Yes,' she beamed. 'I'd like that.'

He grinned. 'So, I have a girlfriend?'

'Yes. And I have a boyfriend?'

'Not just any old boyfriend, the world's best one,' he laughed. 'And I have the world's best girlfriend.' He squeezed her hand.

They smiled warmly at each other. No words were needed to express how happy they both felt.

Remmy and Charlie walked towards them, still swinging their entwined hands.

'Everything good?' Charlie asked.

'We have some news,' Colin said in his sternest voice.

Charlie and Remmy both gave him a concerned frown.

Colin grinned. 'Bridget's now my girlfriend.'

'That's amazing news,' Remmy beamed. 'I'm so excited for you both.'

'You had me going there,' Charlie chuckled. 'But that's great.'

'Thanks, guys,' Bridget smiled.

Remmy was delighted for her friends and even more excited at the prospect of more double dates. Right now, it felt like they were all in a happy, vampire-proof bubble and nothing could burst their happiness.

Chapter Six - Remmy Breaks

Remmy and Sandy were perched at the breakfast bar eating their breakfast when Janice walked into the room clutching her phone.

'Morning girls, you'll never guess who I've just been speaking to?'

'The president?' Sandy snorted.

'No Sandy.' Janice shook her head.

'Grandma Noreen?' Remmy asked before she put a spoonful of cereal into her mouth.

'No sweetheart. It was Catherine, you know, Sydney's mom.'

Remmy choked on her mouthful of cereal and took a quick gulp of her orange juice.

'Remmy, are you okay?' Janice gave her a worried look.

'Yes, Mom, fine thanks.' Remmy forced a smile.

'What did Catherine want?' Sandy asked.

'She asked if you both wanted to stay for another sleepover this Saturday night. Wasn't that lovely of her?'

Remmy gripped onto the side of the breakfast bar. There was no way that she was staying at Sydney's ever again.

'That's cool, we had loads of fun at the last sleepover.' Sandy gave Janice a sickly-sweet smile.

'I know, which is why I told her that you'd both be delighted to stay over.'

'Great,' Sandy grinned.

Remmy went very pale and almost fell off her chair.

'I need to get something from my room,' she muttered, as she hopped off her chair.

When she reached her bedroom, she slumped down onto her bed and placed her head in her hands. She couldn't do it; she couldn't stay at Sydney's again but she'd told the vampires she wouldn't say anything about the prank. If she didn't explain the problem to her mom, how would she get out of going? Maybe she could pretend that she was ill? Was Bridget invited too? If so, could she pretend that she was also ill or would that look too suspicious?

She pulled her phone from her jeans pocket and sent a quick message to Bridget.

>*Have you been invited to Sydney's sleepover too? What do we do?*

She picked at her fingernails as she tried to think of a plan. She was dreading school as the vampires would be talking about the sleepover and making plans. She didn't want to go to Sydney's house ever again and she didn't want to have to spend time with the vampires. They may have pretended to be nice but deep down, Remmy knew she could never trust any of them.

Remmy was about to get up when her phone began to ring. She looked down at the name flashing on the screen. It was Bridget.

'Hey,' she answered.

'I've been invited too,' Bridget whispered. 'What do we do?'

'We should try to keep cool for now and talk about it at school.'

'I can't go to Sydney's again. I won't do it. I won't!'

'I know, I won't either,' Remmy assured her.

'I don't think I can sit there and listen to Sydney's horrible sleepover plans.'

'Tell me about it, I have to sit next to her.'

'I can't do it Remmy,' Bridget replied in a panicky voice.

'I know.' Remmy sighed. We're going to have to tell our mom's, aren't we?'

'Yeah. Can we tell them now?'

'Yeah, I'll tell my mom now. It'll be okay, Bridget.'

'I hope so.'

'Remmy, hurry up or you're going to be late for school,' Janice shouted up the stairs.

'I've got to go. I'll tell my mom now.'

'Okay, Remmy. I'll tell mine too.'

Remmy ended the phone call then took a deep breath. She should have just told her mom about the prank straight away and not allowed Sandy to bully her into staying quiet.

There was a knock at the door. It opened and Janice peered her head around it. 'Remmy, Marcus and Sandy are waiting in the car. What's taking you so long?'

'I'm sorry, Mom,' Remmy sobbed. 'I need to tell you something.'

'Remmy, what's wrong?' Janice walked over and perched down on the bed next to her.

'I can't go to Sydney's sleepover.'

'Why ever not? I thought you had a lovely time there?'

'No, I didn't.' Remmy shook her head. 'They pulled a prank on us and it upset me...and Bridget. We don't want to go back there because we don't feel safe.'

'What kind of prank?' Her mom gave her a quizzing look.

'Sydney's parents said they were going out.'

'They left you in the house alone?' Janice sounded horrified.

'Well, that's what they said. Then we heard a smashing noise and the lights went out and then it sounded like furniture was being moved downstairs. So we all hid in Sydney's walk-in-wardrobe. Sydney said she was going to sneak downstairs to phone for help, so we all sat there terrified and then we heard a scream. Then there were footsteps in the room that were moving towards us. The wardrobe door opened and there were three people in black hoodies standing there. One of them had a knife covered in blood. Then they all pulled their hoods down and laughed. It was Sydney and her parents. Sydney set up the whole thing.'

'Her parents allowed for this to happen and they even joined in with it?'

Remmy nodded her head.

'They had a knife?'

'It was a fake one but it looked so real at the time.'

'Why on earth didn't you tell me about this sooner?' Janice pulled Remmy in for a hug.

'I'm sorry, Mom, I wanted to tell you but Sandy didn't want me to.'

'Why wouldn't she want me to know about this?'

'Because she was worried that if you and Marcus knew what happened then you'd never let us have a sleepover again.'

'Well, I'm not happy that you both lied to me and I know that Marcus won't be happy, either. We just want you both to be safe and when you stay over at someone else's house, we're entrusting you into that family's care. What they did was frightening and uncalled for. You're twelve-year-old girls and that kind of prank is not acceptable behaviour!'

'I can't stay there again, Mom, I can't,' Remmy sobbed.

'I know sweetie; I wouldn't expect you too.' Janice hugged her tighter.

Janice's cardigan itched against Remmy's face but she didn't budge. She felt safe in her mom's embrace and she didn't want it to end.

'Let's go downstairs and talk about this properly. I need to talk to Catherine and then we need to discuss it as a family.'

'But what about school?'

'School will just have to wait for a bit. I'll call the office and let them know that you girls will be late.'

'I'm sorry, Mom.'

'I know, Remmy. I know.'

Remmy followed her mother downstairs and was gestured into the living room. She sat on one of the couches and fiddled with her nails whilst she waited for her mom to return. She wondered how Bridget was getting on? She thought about messaging her but then realized that she'd left her phone upstairs. She heard shouting coming from out in the hallway and recognized Sandy's voice. She heard the words, 'so unfair,' and, 'it's all her fault.' Remmy gulped and sank further into the couch. Eventually, Janice walked into the room along with a stressed looking Marcus and a glum-looking Sandy.

'Loser,' Sandy mouthed to her, as she threw herself onto the other couch.

Remmy stared down at her feet. She knew that she'd done the right thing in telling her mom about the prank. But she really didn't want to have to deal with the backlash she'd now receive from Sandy and the vampires. Still, there was no way that she and Bridget could have coped with another sleepover at Sydney's. Sleepovers were meant to be filled with watching movies and eating too much popcorn, they weren't meant to include fearing for your life.

'It's okay, Remmy.' Janice gave her a warm look as she sat down next to her. 'Neither of you will be going to Sydney's sleepover.'

'This is so unfair!' Sandy folded her arms. 'It was a harmless prank. It's not my fault that *some* people are too sensitive.'

'Sandy, it was a prank that went way too far,' Marcus said sternly.

'Whatever,' Sandy muttered.

'I just called Catherine and explained to her that what she did to a bunch of twelve-year-old-girls was unacceptable and that because of it neither of you would be staying there again,' Janice said.

'What did she say?' Remmy asked.

'She said she couldn't see a problem with the prank.' Janice looked flustered. 'I think it's best if you both stay away from Sydney. Her parents have very different views from Marcus and me.'

'That's not fair,' Sandy protested. 'Sydney's my friend and if I want to stay at her house, then I will!' She jumped to her feet and stomped across the room, tears filling her eyes.

'Cassandra, come back here this instant,' Marcus shouted after her.

'It's all your fault!' Sandy scowled at Remmy before storming out of the room.

Marcus stood up and gave Janice a knowing look as he hurried after Sandy.

Remmy thought that Sandy was being fickle. It wasn't that long ago she was convinced that Sydney was bullying her. Now suddenly they were the best of friends and Remmy felt like an outsider.

'Great, now Sandy hates me.' Remmy leaned her head on her mom's shoulder.

'No, she doesn't, sweetie.' Janice placed her arm around Remmy's shoulder. 'She's just upset, she'll come around.'

'Yeah,' Remmy muttered but she didn't believe her own words.

Sandy and the vampires would be fuming and no good ever came from enraging a member of the living dead.

'You can talk to me, Remmy, I know I'm old and uncool but I love you and I want the best for you.'

'You're not old,' Remmy said to her mom.

'But I suppose I am uncool?' Janice smiled.

'I think you're very cool. You're the best mom ever and I love you. I know I should have told you, I just didn't want to upset Sandy and the others. We've been getting on so much better lately and I didn't want that to change.'

'I know, darling, but this prank sounds very frightening and you shouldn't have had to bottle that up.' Janice rubbed Remmy's back.

Marcus peered around the door and waved the house phone at Janice. 'It's Bridget's mom,' he mouthed.

'I'll be right back.' Janice smiled at Remmy before hurrying over and taking the phone from Marcus.

Remmy watched as they both left the room. Sandy was probably right. Most likely, they wouldn't be allowed out again until they were twenty-one. But on the plus side, at least they didn't have to endure another night at Sydney's mansion of horrors. One thing was for sure...school was going to suck! She was glad that she'd have Bridget there too. Well, she hoped that she would. What if Bridget's mom let her stay home from school? She'd be alone with an angry group of stirred-up vampires. She shuddered at the thought.

By the time Janice walked back into the room ten minutes

later, Remmy had thought through the worst scenarios in her head.

She anxiously tapped her fingers against her lap. 'Is Bridget okay?'

'Yes.' Janice sat down next to Remmy. 'She's a little shaken up but her mom says she's fine.'

Remmy sighed. 'Good.'

'Her mom's also extremely annoyed that it took so long for Bridget to tell her what happened," Janice continued. "I don't think Bridget will be allowed to go to any sleepovers for a while. Bridget said she kept it quiet because of peer pressure. I understand that it's hard growing up and that you want to fit in... but what Sydney's parents did was wrong. If anything like that happens again, you must tell me.'

'I will,' Remmy muttered. 'But, Mom, do I have to go to school today?'

'Yes sweetie,' Janice rubbed her arm. 'Bridget will be at school. Her mom is taking her now.'

'Okay. I guess I'll be alright then,' Remmy mumbled.

'If you have any trouble then talk to me. Let me know.' Janice gave her a reassuring smile.

Remmy nodded in response. "I will."

'Right.' Janice jumped to her feet. 'We'd better not keep Marcus waiting any longer.'

Remmy nodded her head reluctantly. She didn't want to go to school at all, let alone have to tolerate a car journey with Sandy. She knew there was no getting out of it, besides, she couldn't leave Bridget alone to face the wrath of the vampires.

'You'll be fine, Remmy." Her mother tried to convince her once more. 'You did the right thing in telling me. I know you probably think that adults are worriers but it's only because we care about you.'

'I know, Mom,' Remmy stood up.

Her mom smiled at her. 'I love you more than the moon.'

'I love you more than a pony,' Remmy replied.

'I love you more than flowers.'

'I love you more than bears.'

'It'll be okay.' Janice bent down and kissed the top of Remmy's head. 'Now, come on. Marcus is already late for work and he has a meeting in less than an hour.'

Remmy trudged after her. She forced a smile onto her face so she could try to appear upbeat but her body language said otherwise. She grabbed her backpack and walked over to the car where she saw Sandy scowling at her from the passenger seat and Marcus tapping his fingers impatiently against the steering wheel.

'Bye girls, have a good day.' Janice waved from the doorway.

Remmy gave her a small wave in return. 'That's pretty unlikely,' she muttered under her breath.

She got into the back passenger seat and stared out of the window. Sandy kept sighing and huffing as she scrolled through her phone. Remmy tried to convince herself that telling her mom had been the right thing to do. There was no way she could have dealt with going to another Sydney sleepover and she was relieved that she didn't have to keep a secret from her mother any longer. At the same time, she was worried that by telling her mom she'd managed to stir up the vampires. Life was so much easier when they were at (sort-of) friend status. Sandy wouldn't be mad forever, would she? Everything would be fine, wouldn't it?

Remmy was shaken out of her thoughts when Marcus pulled up outside the school.

'I hope you girls have a good day. Don't worry about being late. Janice has already phoned the school and explained.' He fiddled with his shirt cuff as he spoke.

'Thanks, Dad,' Sandy smiled at him as she got out of the car.

Remmy thanked him and stepped onto the pavement but before she'd even closed the car door, Sandy had rushed off ahead. Even though Remmy would have rather walked into class alongside Sandy than being late by herself, she didn't rush after her. She decided that it was best to give Sandy some time to calm down.

Remmy had only taken a couple of steps when she heard a car pull up behind her. Thinking that it was Marcus returning she turned around. She gave a relieved smile when she saw Bridget hop out of her mom's car. Bridget hurried over to her. Her eyes were red from crying and her hair was tangled from sticking to her wet cheeks.

'I'm glad you're here, I was feeling really scared about walking into class on my own,' Bridget said.

'Same, Sandy ran off as soon as the car stopped.'

'Is she mad at you?'

'Super mad but she'll get over it.' Remmy gave her friend a

half-hearted smile.

'I hope so.'

'They all will. Well, I'm not so sure about Sydney, but hopefully, she will eventually. I don't want anyone to be mad, I just don't want to go to any more of Sydney's sleepovers. I'm still having nightmares about the last one.'

'Me too.' Bridget blushed. 'But don't tell anyone.'

'Of course, I won't. Don't tell anyone about me, either.'

'Definitely not! But the vampires are going to be really mad.'

'It'll be okay, we have each other,' Remmy smiled at her friend.

'I know. And now we don't have to go to any more of Sydney's sleepovers!'

'Thank goodness for that! Now, come on!' Remmy grabbed Bridget's arm. 'We can do this.'

Bridget gave an agreeing nod. As they walked up the empty hallways, Remmy found herself thinking about her first day here, back when she'd got lost and Amelia had helped her. She had come so far since then, so she knew that she could handle whatever the vampires threw at her. Back then, she hadn't known anyone, but now she had Bridget, Charlie, Mike, and Colin. She wasn't alone. She belonged at this school. She wasn't a weak person...she was strong.

They stopped in front of their classroom door and looked at each other.

'Are you ready?' she whispered to Bridget.

'I don't know if I can do this.' The color had left her cheeks and she clutched her churning stomach.

'You can.' Remmy gave her a reassuring smile. 'We both can.'

Bridget took a big gulp of breath. 'Okay.'

Together they both pushed open the door and stepped into the room.

Chapter Seven - It's Happening Again

Everyone in the classroom turned and stared, including the teacher, who had fallen silent.

'Oh! Hello girls.' She sounded flustered. 'Please take your seats.'

Remmy could feel Sandy's glare burning into her. She hoped Sandy wouldn't be mad at her for too long but she knew they probably wouldn't be besties for quite some time. As she neared her desk, she could see how furious Sydney looked. Remmy gave her a small smile as she placed her backpack down on top of her desk and then quickly glanced away.

As Remmy sat down and pulled in her chair, Sydney locked eyes with her. 'You're dead!' she mouthed.

Remmy gulped and cast her eyes downwards. She knew Sydney would be mad but that was no excuse to threaten her. It just added to the list of things that her mom would want her to talk about, but which she knew she probably wouldn't. She tried to compose herself by taking in a deep breath.

She looked at Sydney, who was now doodling a heart on her piece of paper. 'I'm sorry,' Remmy whispered.

'Whatever!' Sydney rolled her eyes.

Remmy gulped again. Miss Sutherland frowned at them and Remmy slumped further down in her seat. She would talk to Sydney at break time and try to explain why she and Bridget had told their moms about the prank. Hopefully, Sydney would understand when she got over her initial annoyance. Isn't that what would happen? Sydney was her friend, wasn't she?

The first lesson of the day seemed to drone on (even though Remmy had missed some of it) but by the time it had finished, an anxious feeling had crawled into Remmy's stomach. She didn't want to explain to the other kids why they were late and she didn't want to talk to Sydney and the vampires. She just wanted to return home and climb into bed.

Most of the kids hurried out of the classroom but Remmy lingered behind. Sydney wasn't in a rush either, she was still doodling.

'Sydney.' The word came out as a squeak causing Remmy to wince. She coughed to clear her voice. 'Um, Sydney?'

'What!' Sydney snarled at her.

'Um, can we um, talk please?'

'No!' Sydney snapped. 'I don't want to talk to you, you're nothing but a horrible little snitch and I hate you!'

She gave Remmy a death stare before swiping her sheet of notepaper into her backpack. She then stood up and then stormed over to the vampires who were waiting for her by the door.

'What was all that about?' Charlie gave Remmy a confused look as he walked over to her with Bridget and Colin.

Remmy blushed. 'Oh, nothing,'

Colin grinned. 'Has anyone ever told you that you're a terrible liar.'

'I'm not lying.' Remmy chewed on the side of her lip. 'Sydney's in a bit of a mood because we aren't going to her sleepover, that's all.'

'That sucks. Why can't you go?' Charlie asked.

Bridget felt uncomfortable talking about this, so she looked away.

'We've just got other plans.'

Charlie shrugged. 'Well, I'm sure she'll get over it. If you have other plans then you have other plans, she should understand that.'

'Yeah,' Remmy muttered.

'What do girls do at sleepovers anyway? Is it all pillow fights and talking about boys?' Colin asked, smirking.

'Pretty much,' Remmy giggled.

'Oh, really! Did you talk about me?' Colin looked at Bridget.

'No.' Bridget blushed. 'I mean, maybe.'

'Of course, you talked about me. I mean what's not to talk about.' He pointed his thumbs towards his chest. 'After all, I'm awesome.'

'Come on, stop embarrassing Bridget and let's go and get some food, I'm starving,' Charlie laughed.

As they walked out of the classroom, Colin edged himself next to Bridget. 'Are you okay, girlfriend?'

She looked up at him and chuckled. 'I'm good, boyfriend,'

Remmy found herself smiling. Today might not have started in the best way but she was happy that her friends had finally got together. They walked into the cafeteria and Remmy and Bridget headed towards Mike's table as Charlie and Colin joined the queue. As the girls passed by the vampires' table, they noticed that Sydney was sitting with them. Sydney and the vampires all death-stared Remmy and Bridget and giggled as they walked past. Although this made the two girls feel uncomfortable, Remmy linked her arm through Bridget's and they tried their best to ignore the smirking behavior.

Mike was mid-bite through a chocolate muffin as they sat down at his table. He gave them a wave and crumbs fell down onto his t-shirt. The girls tried not to laugh as he peered down at his top and quickly wiped the crumbs off. With their backs to the vampires' table, they felt less intimidated but were both aware that the group was most likely still glaring at them.

'How come you were late to class?' Mike asked before he placed the last piece of his muffin into his mouth.

Both girls exchanged looks. Should they tell the boys the truth or keep it to themselves? Would the boys think they were chickens if they heard what happened? Or would they understand why the girls were upset? Would sharing the details cause more issues with the vampires? Remmy felt overwhelmed. The day had been a stressful one and it was still only morning.

'Car trouble,' she muttered. 'And Bridget's mom couldn't find her car keys.'

'So, you both had car trouble?' Mike raised an eyebrow.

'Yeah, it took my mom forever to find her keys. They were in the pocket of the jeans she wore yesterday,' Bridget quickly added.

'Fair enough, at least you both got to miss part of our morning class.'

'Yeah.' Remmy smiled awkwardly while Bridget quickly looked away.

Charlie and Colin appeared with trays of food and drink and placed them down on the table.

'I got you a chocolate milk.' Charlie pushed it along the table towards Remmy.

'Thanks, Charlie.' She beamed at him gratefully.

Colin grinned at Bridget. 'I got you a chocolate milk and a muffin.'

'Okay, some of us have to budget our canteen money,' Charlie chuckled as he smiled at Remmy. 'But I'll happily share my chocolate bar with you.'

'Really?' Colin looked shocked. 'Charlie's sharing his chocolate. It's official, he must REALLY like you.' He smirked at Remmy.

'Yeah!' Charlie grinned. 'I guess I do.'

'Bleurgh!' Bridget moved her fingers up to her mouth and pretended to be sick.

'Like you can talk,' Mike mocked.

Remmy blushed as she looked down at the chocolate milk. Charlie never shared his food, so the fact that he'd offered to give her half of his chocolate bar...meant that he must really like her. She liked him too. A lot! He was the first boy she had ever really liked. Just a glimpse of him made her smile, and spending time with him made her happy. Even with all the vampire drama going on, being around Charlie and her friends made her feel like she belonged. Sydney could be mean and malicious but she didn't have what Remmy had, she didn't have true friends.

'Here you go.' Charlie held out the remaining half of the chocolate still sitting in the wrapper.

'Thanks.' Remmy took it from him with a smile.

'I wouldn't share my chocolate bar with anyone,' Mike said.

'That's because you haven't got a girlfriend. Give it time.' Colin patted him on the shoulder. 'Hey Bridge, do you have any single friends?'

She grinned. 'Sophie's single.'

'No chance,' Mike snorted.

'She's a nice girl,' Bridget commented.

Yeah, but she makes annoying comments. Did you hear her in class this morning when Miss Sutherland was trying to help her with her math? She went on and on about how her pet gerbil wasn't using its ball.'

'It's a big concern,' Colin sniggered.

'Shut it.' Mike couldn't hide his grin as he shook his head.

Sydney was walking past their table when she pretended to trip and her half-full milkshake spilled down the back of Bridget's white t-shirt. Bridget squealed and jumped up to her feet.

'I'm so sorry.' Sydney gave her a look that said…'I'm seriously concerned.' She shook her head. 'I am sooo clumsy.'

Bridget tried to peer over her shoulder to see the damage but she couldn't make it out properly. Remmy rushed to her feet and started dabbing at Bridget's back with napkins.

'Is it bad?' Bridget asked Remmy.

'It'll be fine.'

'Here.' Charlie passed her more napkins.

'Thanks.' Remmy smiled at Charlie.

'It was an accident.' Sydney couldn't hide the smirk that played at the corners of her lips. 'And it's barely noticeable.'

'Come on Bridge, let's go to the bathroom and see if we can get rid of the stain.' Remmy grabbed Bridget's hand and pulled her up. Bridget nodded and then bit down on her lip so that she didn't cry. Even though Remmy walked slightly behind her to try and hide her milkshake stained top, she could see people looking and sniggering at the brown mark.

Bridget's day had certainly had its ups and downs, but now she had to spend the rest of the day dressed in a chocolate milk stained top.

In the bathroom, Remmy grabbed some paper towels and dampened them before she gently scrubbed at the stains. The wet sections of the t-shirt turned transparent and stuck to Bridget's skin but the stains didn't fade.

'It's no good.' Bridget sighed as she walked over to the hand dryer. 'I'm just going to have to look stupid all day.'

'You don't look stupid.' Remmy raised her voice so she could be heard over the sound of the hand dryer.

Sophie burst into the room and hurried over to them. Bridget rolled her eyes and then focused the heat from the dryer onto her t-shirt.

'I saw what happened,' Sophie shouted. 'I feel sooo bad for you, I mean, how embarrassing to be stuck in a brown stained top all day!' she shuddered.

'It's not that bad,' Remmy said.

'It's terrible!' Sophie shuddered again. 'Anyway, I'm here to save the day. I always come prepared, whatever the weather.' She pulled her backpack from her back and rummaged through it.

Bridget gave Remmy a 'help me' glare. This situation was bad enough without Sophie making her feel even worse. Remmy gave a sympathetic look in return before glancing at Sophie. The hand dryer stopped and Bridget folded her arms and willed back her tears.

'Thanks Sophie, but I think Bridget needs some time alone.'

'Ah, there it is.' She pulled out a cream cardigan with small pink and red hearts on it. 'You can borrow this.' She held it out to Bridget.

'Thanks, Sophie,' Bridget smiled as she took it from her. 'And sorry for being grumpy.'

Sophie shrugged. 'That's okay, I'd be the same if I was covered in chocolate milk. Anyway, I'll catch you both in class.' She waved a quick goodbye and left the bathroom.

Bridget put the cardigan on and then looked at herself in the long, rectangular mirror that was attached to the wall above the sinks.

'Do I look stupid?'

'Nope.' Remmy tried to hide her grin as she shook her head.

'Then why are you laughing?'

'I'm not laughing. Honestly, you look fine and at least it covers the chocolate milk,' Remmy replied.

'I guess. But it's such a warm day, I'm going to melt.'

'You'll be fine.'

'You know that I'm no good with heat.' Bridget wiped the sweat off her forehead. 'I'll be a lobster by lunchtime.'

'You can have an ice block at lunch to cool you down.'

'Maybe.' Bridget frowned. 'Do you think Sydney spilled it on purpose?'

'I don't know.' Remmy bit on her lip. 'She said it was an accident, so it probably was.'

'Yeah, maybe.' Bridget looked at the floor. 'I guess we'd better get to class; we've already been late once today.'

'Come on then.' Remmy placed her arm around Bridget's shoulders and led her towards the door.

'Are you sure that I look okay?'

'Yes, you look fine,' Remmy reassured her.

When they walked into the classroom most of the other kids were already sitting in their seats but Miss Sutherland was nowhere to be seen. News of the milkshake incident had spread and everyone stared at Bridget as she walked over to her desk.

'Nice cardigan,' Rach sniggered, which caused the rest of the vampires to laugh.

'You honestly look fine. Ignore them,' Remmy whispered to her friend.

Bridget sat down and stared at her desk. She was sweltering in the cardigan but she knew she couldn't take it off. One thing was for sure, it was going to be a long day!

Remmy sat down on her chair and tapped her fingers against her desk. She peered at the back of Charlie's head and found herself daydreaming about him. She stopped tapping her fingers and leaned her head on her upright arm. His messy hair was so cute and he had an amazing smile and his eyes were so beautiful, she could easily stare into them all day…

Suddenly she was tumbling and found herself landing with a *thud* on the floor. Sydney was standing there, a wide smirk plastered to her face. She'd pulled Remmy's chair out from under her. The vampires burst out laughing and Remmy felt her cheeks reddening. Charlie rushed over and helped her up to her feet.

'Remmy, are you okay?' He looked concerned.

'Yeah, I'm okay.' She sounded flustered.

'You shouldn't have done that!' Charlie glared at Sydney. 'It was dangerous!'

'Whatever!' Sydney rolled her eyes. 'It was just a bit of fun.'

'She could have been hurt.'

'*She could have been hurt,*' Sydney mimicked him.

'You're so immature.'

'Guys, it's okay. I'm okay.' Remmy tried to diffuse the situation.

'Get a life, Charlie, stop being a fun killer.' Sydney folded her arms.

'How would you like it if someone pulled that stunt on you?' Charlie demanded.

'I wouldn't be stupid enough to let it happen,' Sydney replied.

Miss Sutherland walked into the room and everyone fell silent. Charlie gave Sydney one last glare before returning to his seat. Remmy repositioned her chair then pulled it in close to her desk. She tried to avoid looking at Sydney as she didn't want to see her smug face. One thing was for sure, it seemed highly likely that she'd spilled her milkshake over Bridget on purpose.

'So, class, I have a fun activity for you to do,' Miss Sutherland announced. 'Each of you will be given one of these flowers.' She held up a paper flower with four petals on it. 'In your allocated pairs you are to write down four positive things about each other and then you'll read them out to the rest of the class.'

Remmy looked over at Bridget eagerly, this sounded like a great idea for them to cheer each other up. Miss Sutherland knew that they were best friends so she had to pair them together, right?

'Let's see.' She looked across the room. 'Susie, you can be paired with Sophie.'

'What!' Susie gave an unimpressed look.

'Colin and Mike. Bridget and Rach.'

Bridget looked horrified. Yes, her day was definitely going from bad to worse. How on earth was she meant to think up four nice things to say about Rach? She could think of four mean things easily enough, *bully, cruel, mean* and *vicious*. Thinking up four nice things about someone so mean wouldn't be easy.

'Remmy can go with Sydney,' Miss Sutherland smiled. 'And neither of you will have to move.'

Remmy's stomach sank. No, no, no, no, no, she couldn't be paired up with the girl who'd just pulled her chair out from under her and embarrassed her in front of the whole class. This was the worst situation ever!!!

Miss Sutherland finished pairing up the class. 'Can one person from each pair please come up here to collect the flowers.'

Sydney scraped back her chair and gave Remmy a devious smirk as she made her way over to the teacher's desk. Remmy sank further into her seat and tried to think up four nice things to say about someone she didn't like or trust. Was being a good prankster a compliment or an insult? Crazy parents definitely weren't something nice, nor was being a diva. She tried to think of positive words to describe Sydney; this was going to be a real challenge.

Sydney returned with two paper flowers. She passed Remmy the baby pink one and placed the crumpled-up brown one down on her own desk.

'This is going to be so much fun.' Sydney smirked as she wrote a word down on one of the petals.

Remmy sighed. 'Yeah, it's going to be great.'

Sydney wrote down her four words quickly, then turned over her flower so Remmy couldn't sneak a look at it. Remmy gave her a cautious look, she didn't trust her at all and was worried about what Sydney had written. The words would be read out in front of the whole class so Sydney wouldn't have said anything bad, would she?

'It's going to be such a lovely surprise for you,' Sydney grinned at her.

Remmy stared down at her petals. So far, she'd come up with two positive words to describe Sydney and she was struggling to think up any more. This would have been so easy if she'd been paired with Bridget. Too easy, which was probably why Miss Sutherland had teamed her with Sydney.

'Five more minutes,' Miss Sutherland addressed the class.

Remmy felt herself begin to panic, she needed to think up two more positive words and quickly. Sydney was confident, which was positive. Remmy wrote down the word *confident* on one of the petals. She took a quick glance at Sydney, who was always immaculately dressed. She scribbled down the word *fashionable*. She flipped over her flower with a relieved smile on her face.

Bridget was stressing out. Coming up with four positive words to describe Rach wasn't easy and so far, she'd only managed one. Worse still, Rach had finished her flower and had her hands pressed over it as she sat with a satisfied expression filling her features.

As she chewed on the end of her pen, Bridget looked around the classroom. Most of the kids had finished, including Remmy, who smiled over at her. If Remmy could come up with four positive words about Sydney, then surely Bridget could think of some positive words about Rach. She quickly jotted down the first two nice words that popped into her head. Then she tried hard to think up one more.

Miss Sutherland scanned the room. 'That's enough time, now, we'll go around the class and each of you can read out your positive words.'

Bridget felt sick, she didn't want to get into trouble for not finishing her task. She could hardly tell the teacher that she hadn't finished because Rach was a mean horrible person who didn't have many good qualities.

'You'd better hurry up or you'll end up in detention for a month,' Rach scoffed.

Bridget felt flustered. Rach thought she was so witty. Witty, that could be a positive thing, couldn't it? She jotted it down on her last petal and then gave Rach a large smile.

As each pair stood up and read out their words, Remmy found herself smiling. So far, everyone had been very kind about their partner. Mike had described Colin as *funny, clever, great friend* and *kind*. Colin had described Mike as *creative, brave, loyal* and *determined*. Even Susie had managed to be nice about Sophie by using the words *original, unique, quirky* and *cheerful*. Sophie had described Susie as *smart, friendly, happy* and *funny*. Remmy didn't think that those words suited Susie but at least Sophie had tried to be nice.

'Remmy and Sydney, can you please stand up.' Miss Sutherland looked at them.

Remmy stood up and nervously glanced at her flower, while Sydney stood with confidence and pressed her flower to her chest.

'Remmy, please go first,' Miss Sutherland instructed her.

Remmy coughed to clear her throat. Then she began. 'Four positive words to describe Sydney are *beautiful, intelligent, confident* and *fashionable.*'

Sydney gave her a smug look which made Remmy feel uncomfortable. She had no idea what Sydney had written on her flower.

'My four words to describe Remmy are *average, follower, organized* and *handsome boyfriend.*' She spoke without looking down at her flower. Looking pleased with herself, she sat back down.

The vampires sniggered and some of the other kids laughed but most of the class remained silent. Charlie shook his head and muttered the word, 'nasty'.

Remmy remained on her feet, a dismayed look on her face. She knew that Sydney was a mean girl but she could have at least tried to think of some nice words. Each word she had used to describe Remmy was plain and dull. The only positive word was handsome and that was to describe Charlie.

'Thank you, girls.' Miss Sutherland sounded unimpressed.

Remmy sat back down and deliberately avoided looking at Sydney. She made sure that she had a smile forced on her face so that the other kids wouldn't think Sydney had upset her. Still, the thoughts lingered in her head. Was she really plain and dull? Was it really that difficult to think of positive words to describe her? Did everyone secretly agree with Sydney? She tried to shake these thoughts away. Sydney wanted this...she wanted Remmy to be filled with negativity. Remmy didn't want to give her the satisfaction of knowing that she had upset her.

When it was time for Bridget and Rach to have their turn, they both stood up and looked down at their flowers. Bridget was worried that her words weren't positive enough. Even though she didn't like Rach, she still wanted to be nice.

'The four words I have to describe Rach are *pretty, popular, loyal friend* and *witty.*'

She looked at Rach to determine her reaction but her face was expressionless. Were those words okay or had they not been positive enough?

'My four words to describe Bridget are *quiet, rule-abiding, orange and academic,*' Rach announced smugly.

A few of the other kids chuckled when Rach read out the word *orange* and all of the vampires were sneering. But Bridget's friends gave Rach stern looks. They didn't think what she had done was funny, instead, they thought it was cruel.

'Okay.' Miss Sutherland sighed. 'Please sit down girls.'

Bridget turned and looked at Remmy and they both rolled their eyes and shook their heads. Remmy knew that Bridget was so much more than the words Rach had used, so she tried to convince herself that she was far better than the words that Sydney had used for her. Sydney's opinion didn't matter, nor did any of the vampires. They weren't her friends and there was a good reason for that. Friends were meant to support you and make you feel better about yourself, not put you down or get a kick out of saying mean things to you.

Miss Sutherland asked everyone to place their flowers on a display stand at the front of the class. Remmy grimaced as she saw Sydney place hers so that it was the most visible. Miss Sutherland then talked about positivity and how important it was to be kind to each other.

The bell sounded and Remmy was the first up out of her seat. Finally, it was lunchtime.

'Remmy, Sydney, Rach, and Bridget, please can you stay behind for a quick word,' Miss Sutherland said, looking at each of the girls.

Remmy sank back down into her seat and sighed. So much for a quick getaway, this day really was turning out to be super lame. Everyone else left the room while the four girls walked over to Miss Sutherland's desk. Remmy and Bridget exchanged worried looks. Surely they couldn't be in trouble, could they?

'So, girls, I've asked you to stay behind because I'm disappointed. Sydney and Rachel, I don't think that the words you chose to describe Bridget and Remmy were particularly positive.'

'They were the best words that I could come up with,' Sydney replied.

'Yeah, I struggled to come up with nice words to describe Bridget because we aren't friends,' Rach remarked.

Both Remmy and Bridget fought back tears, Sydney and

Rachel's comments stung. Still, they were determined not to give them the satisfaction of crying in front of them.

'Okay, girls,' Miss Sutherland sounded flustered. 'The whole point of this activity was to be positive.' She took the four flowers off the display then handed each of the girls a new flower. 'Remmy, you can pair up with Bridget, and Rachel, you can pair up with Sydney. You can all go off to lunch once you've finished.'

Remmy and Bridget nodded but Sydney and Rach looked annoyed.

'This is so unfair,' Sydney muttered under her breath.

'Is there a problem?' Miss Sutherland looked at her sternly.

'Not at all.' Sydney forced a fake smile.

Remmy didn't think it was fair that she and Bridget had to stay when they'd managed to write down positive comments. Though, she didn't tell Miss Sutherland this. While it was unfair, part of her was relieved that Sydney's flower with the words she'd written about Remmy had been removed. At the same time, she couldn't help thinking that if Miss Sutherland had paired her up with Bridget in the first place the whole situation would have been avoided.

'I'm so hungry.' Bridget placed her hand to her stomach as it gurgled. 'I hope they don't run out of cheese fries.'

Remmy smiled. 'This won't take long. It's easy to think up positive comments about you.'

'Likewise.' Bridget smiled back before she quickly jotted a word down on one of her petals.

Remmy wrote down *happy, smart, caring and amazing friend.* She showed the flower to Bridget and then wrapped her arms around her.

'You're the best friend ever,' Remmy said.

'Here.' Bridget passed Remmy the flower she'd written on. Bridget had written down the words *friendly, kind, thoughtful* and *super-fast*.

'Thanks,' Remmy grinned at her. 'And thanks for being my best friend.'

'Always!' Bridget beamed.

They both took their flowers over to Miss Sutherland.

'That was quick!' She read the words and smiled. 'How lovely, you can both go to lunch.'

Remmy and Bridget walked happily across the room. Sydney and Rach both scowled at them. They still hadn't finished writing positive words about each other.

'Girls, wait,' Miss Sutherland called out.

Both Remmy and Bridget paused by the door, worried looks had replaced their smiles.

'Is everything okay?' Miss Sutherland asked them quietly.

Remmy looked over at Sydney, who was glaring back at her.

'Everything's fine, Miss.' Remmy smiled half-heartedly.

'Bridget?' Miss Sutherland looked at her.

'Yes, fine,' Bridget replied.

'Well, if you're sure?' When both girls nodded, she spoke again. 'If you have any problems, let me know.'

'We will,' Remmy said.

Remmy and Bridget exchanged a look before they left the classroom.

'Do you think we should have told her?' Bridget asked.

'I think that would have made it worse,' Remmy sighed.

'I guess.' Bridget looked worried.

'Don't worry.' Remmy gave her a reassuring smile. 'They'll soon get bored with teasing us.'

'They'll find someone else to suck the blood out of,' Bridget chuckled.

'Exactly.'

Remmy kept the smile on her face but secretly she was worried, too She knew how relentless Sandy and her friends could be. She'd already been on the receiving end of many of their mean actions. They weren't the type of girls to drop things and move on easily, instead, they held on to negatives and took delight in hurting people's feelings. Worse still, they now had Sydney as a member and she seemed even more devious than the others. Even Sandy wouldn't have gone as far as Sydney's sleepover prank. Remmy had a bad feeling that the vampires were far from finished with their tormenting behaviour. She just hoped she was wrong.

***

The rest of the day passed by smoothly, apart from some mean looks and sniggers in their direction, the vampires left them alone. Sydney was now a fully-fledged member of the vampires. She sat with them at break times and completely avoided her old group. Remmy found it odd that Sandy had gone from despising her to liking her so quickly. Then again, that was the vampires for you, they were fickle. Still, Remmy was dreading going home and having to act nicely towards Sandy around the house. She wanted to be able to go home and escape her, not have to be friendly over dinner.

As she left the library and walked along the empty hallway,

her conflict with the vampires played on her mind. She longed to be able to talk to Amelia about it as she always gave the best advice. Remmy continued walking until she reached the bench where she always used to meet Amelia. She sat down and sighed as she hugged her backpack. There was no one around so it seemed unlikely that Amelia was going to appear...

'Hey, girlfriend.'

Remmy looked up and saw Amelia smiling back at her. She stared at her open-mouthed, not quite believing that she was real. Of course, she'd appeared, Amelia had a knack of appearing exactly when Remmy needed her to.

'Hey,' Remmy mumbled.

'That's not the welcome I was hoping for,' Amelia laughed.

'S-sorry, I just wasn't expecting you to be here. Though I sat here in the hope that you would.'

'I'm always here for you.' Amelia sat down next to her. 'What's up?'

'Everything's going great with Charlie, and Bridget's got a boyfriend. He's called Colin and he's super funny. They make the cutest couple; it's so good to see them happy.'

Amelia raised an eyebrow. 'That's great Remmy...but I know something's worrying you. What is it?'

'Okay,' Remmy sighed. 'There is something. It's the vampires, they now have a new member. Sydney. I think she might be even worse than Sandy. Sydney's family are crazy as well. I think Sydney was bullying Sandy, then we had a sleepover at her place and she played this horrible prank on us that wasn't funny at all. It really scared Bridget and me. We told our moms about it and now the vampires are mad at us, and they're not being very nice. Today, Sydney spilled her chocolate milkshake down the back of Bridget's top. She even pulled my chair out from under me.'

'It seems as though you've had quite an eventful time.' Amelia wrapped her arm around Remmy's shoulder. 'But you're strong and smart and you have a kind heart. You're my girl and I'm proud of how far you've come.'

'Thanks.' Remmy blushed. 'I couldn't have done it without you.'

'I gave you a gentle guide in the right direction, that's all. You did all the hard work and it's you who always figures out what you should do.'

'I guess.' Remmy bit down on her lip, willing herself not to cry.

'It's true,' Amelia smiled at Remmy. 'Now, what do you think is the best way to deal with this Sydney?'

'Um, I should be wary of her and try to keep my distance as much as possible but still remain friendly and not let her see that she's bothering me.'

Amelia grinned. 'See, girl, you've got it!'

'Thanks, Amelia.'

'Remmy, never stop believing in yourself because you are amazing.'

Remmy leaned over and wrapped her arms around Amelia. Seeing Amelia had made her feel so much better about everything.

'Thank you, Amelia.' Remmy pulled away. 'I'd better go, I have to be at the boardwalk soon, I have a double date.'

'See, you've got things sorted, girl. I bet Sydney isn't going on double dates.'

'No, she's probably gossiping with the rest of the vampires,' Remmy laughed. 'Thank you, not just for this but for everything.'

'Anytime,' Amelia smiled. 'Now go and have fun with your cute boyfriend and awesome friends.'

'You should come, there'll be ice cream and we could get shakes and you can meet my friends.'

'I would love to but an assignment is calling me. Now, go and have fun.'

'Will do!' Remmy gave Amelia a wave and a large smile before she walked off.

She reached the end of the hallway and peered back at the bench but Amelia had already disappeared.

Chapter Eight - Aww So Romantic!

Remmy jumped off the bus and hurried over to her three friends who were sitting on the boardwalk wall. She noticed that Bridget was in a clean t-shirt (which she'd quickly grabbed from home) and she wasn't in Sophie's heart print cardigan anymore.

'Sorry I'm late,' Remmy said, as she ran up to them.

'You've missed out on a treat,' Colin grinned. 'We've been talking about what words we'd use to describe Sydney and Rach,'

'They're bossy,' Bridget smiled.

'And self-obsessed,' Colin pouted as he struck a pose.

'And vain,' Bridget chuckled.

'And jealous, which is why they felt the need to be so mean in the first place,' Charlie said.

Remmy felt flustered. She was uncomfortable talking about the vampires. They'd tried to ruin her day but they hadn't succeeded because she was with her friends and she was happy.

'Guys, I'm so hungry, can we please go and get ice creams?' She looked at them eagerly.

'Sounds good to me.' Bridget linked her arm through Remmy's.

Charlie grinned. 'As if I'd ever turn down ice cream!'

'Same, especially when it's with my beautiful girlfriend,' Colin smiled.

Bridget blushed and looked down at her feet to try and hide the flush on her skin. Although she liked it when Colin complimented her as it made her feel special, she didn't know how to stop herself from turning so red.

They bought ice creams from a van close to the boardwalk then sat down on the boardwalk wall. Remmy licked her ice cream as she watched the runners and people with rollerblades whizz past. Charlie shuffled closer to Remmy and smiled at her in between gulping down his ice cream.

'I hope you didn't take Sydney's words to heart. You know she's full of rubbish talk, well, apart from me being handsome.' Charlie gave her a genuine encouraging smile. 'You really are amazing; I could have filled a hundred flowers with compliments about you. In fact, ...'

Bridget squealed excitedly and both Remmy and Charlie turned and looked at her. She was clutching one of the paper flowers from class but on it were written positive words about her.

'I asked Miss Sutherland for a blank one then I wrote down some words that I think describe my girlfriend,' Colin said.

'That's so special,' Remmy smiled at her two friends. 'What words are on there, Bridget?'

A blushing Bridget passed over the flower. Remmy looked down at the petals which had the words *beautiful, intelligent, kind* and *interesting* written on each one.

Bridget beamed at Colin. 'Thank you!'

'You don't need to thank me; those words describe the real you and that's why we all think you're amazing.'

Remmy grinned. 'Colin's right, you're the best!'

Bridget continued to blush as she studied her flower. Colin stretched out his arm and placed it around her shoulders. This made her blush even more. She glanced at Remmy who smiled back at her. Remmy was so happy for her friends and so pleased that the day had ended on a good note.

'I have something for you, Remmy.' Charlie pulled a paper flower out of his pocket and passed it to Remmy. 'Colin wasn't the only one to ask Miss Sutherland for an extra flower.'

'Oh my gosh, thank you, Charlie!' Remmy turned almost as red as Bridget had.

The flower was slightly scrunched up from being in his pocket and the words were scrawled in Charlie's messy handwriting but Remmy still thought it was the sweetest gesture ever! She looked down at the words and couldn't hide her smile.

'You're *caring, smart, beautiful* and *funny* to name just a few things. You're such a great person, Remmy and no one ever has the right to put you down.'

Tears of happiness trickled down Remmy's cheeks. She brushed them quickly away.

'Have I upset you?' Charlie looked concerned.

'No.' Remmy shook her head. 'I'm just so happy.'

'You're amazing!' He placed his hand over hers.

Remmy's fingers tingled beneath his. He really was the best boyfriend ever and she felt so lucky to have him. The vampires didn't matter anymore because she had friends to cheer her up and remind her why they liked her. She was a good person with a good heart who deserved to have such great friends.

'You're all such incredible friends,' she sniffed. 'The best friends in the whole wide world and I'm so lucky to have you all.'

'Stop this right now. I didn't bring any tissues,' Colin laughed.

Bridget smiled at her. 'We're lucky to have you, too.'

'Yep, you're the best.' Charlie squeezed her hand.

'Bridget, would you like to leave this soppy pair alone and go for a walk with me?' Colin stood up and held his hand out to her.

'I'd like that.' Bridget blushed as she took his hand and he pulled her up to her feet.

As they walked along the boardwalk, side by side, Colin reached out and took Bridget's hand. She couldn't hide her smile and turned and gave Remmy an excited look.

Charlie looked at Remmy. 'It's great to see them so happy.'

'Yes, it is!' She beamed back at him.

'Remmy, I do really like you.' Charlie looked directly into her eyes. 'You're so wonderful.'

Remmy felt her cheeks redden and her heartbeat pound inside her. She looked back into his eyes and felt her stomach flip.

He leaned in closer to her, his lips nearing hers. This was it...she was going to have her first kiss.

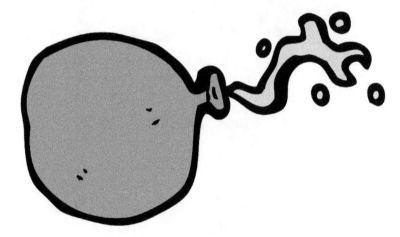

SPLASH!!!

A huge water bomb fell from the sky and exploded all over them.

***

Did you enjoy this story!

It was <u>definitely</u> my fave one to write <u>for</u> you.

What do you think about the prank???

And who threw the water bomb?

Yep, bet you guessed it right!

Find out what happens next in Book 9 – Stop It!

Thank you for reading The Sleepover.

If you could kindly leave a review

it would be greatly appreciated!!!

Katrina x

Some other books you may enjoy...

Just click on the covers below to check them out.

CPSIA information can be obtained
at www.ICGtesting.com
Printed in the USA
FSHW010957180119
55094FS